# Family Secrets

A Pride and Prejudice Variation

*^*^*

Karen Kate Rowley

eBook ASIN: B0C6H6P3KW
Paperback ASIN: B0C6BTJ65C
ISBN: 9798396232815

Cover design by: Karen Kate Rowley

# Contents

# Prologue

*April 14, 1795*

In the dimly lit chamber, a man made his way to his wife's bedside. With delicate precision, he held a tray of tea in his hands, ensuring its equilibrium as the door softly closed behind him.

A heavy shroud of darkness enveloped the room, the curtains tightly drawn, admitting but a slender sliver of light that cast a feeble glow upon the verdant tapestry beneath his feet. His cherished wife, worn by the arduous labour of delivering their fourth daughter, now languished in the clutches of violent illness. Each visit to her sickbed revealed a further ebbing of her vitality, her life force inexorably slipping away, a sight that filled him with trepidation.

Placing the tray on a small table, he assumed his position at Jannie's side, attuned to the laboured wheezing of her breath. Pale and emaciated, her dishevelled tresses clinging to her clammy brow, she appeared a mere shadow of her former self. At that moment, Thomas sensed the looming spectre of his dear wife's impending demise. Unable to restrain his grief, he surrendered to tears, their salty rivulets tracing sorrowful paths down his cheeks. Though he endeavoured to be discreet, the tender sound of his weeping stirred Jannie from her stupor, her eyes fluttering open.

Witnessing her husband's desolation, she spoke in a voice bereft of its customary vigour, her words a whisper on the wind, "My dearest Thom, you must carry on in my absence," she murmured weakly, her voice a rasp. "You must find solace in believing life shall persist for you and our girls. I shall forever cherish and watch over you all."

"Pray, do not speak thus, Jannie!" cried he with fervour, his anguish unbounded. "Do not utter words that suggest our paths shall never converge again! How am I to continue this existence without you? I beseech you, do not leave us!"

Jannie Bennet extended a trembling hand to caress her husband's unshaven cheek, a silent balm to his anguished soul. "Hush, my love," she gently soothed him.

Clasping her hand tightly, he clung to her as if holding onto life itself.

"You must promise me, Thom," implored she, her gaze intense as she met his eyes, her words punctuated by heavy breaths. "Promise me that your grief shall not consume you for too long and that you shall seek solace in the embrace of a new wife, giving a new mother to our girls."

The man shook his head in dissent, unable to fathom such a notion.

"Promise me this, Thom," persisted she. "I must find comfort in knowing that our precious daughters shall be loved, cared for, and guided by a motherly presence throughout their young lives..." Her words trailed off, unshed tears welling in her weary eyes. "Please, Thom, promise me our girls shall have a mother," she whispered, her voice fragile and faint.

Though the weight of his sorrow shattered Mr Bennet, he uttered the words she sought. "I promise."

Suddenly, her grip tightened, her gaze intent as she spoke, her words eclipsed by the laborious rhythm of her breaths, "I must tell you something—about me—I am not—" began she, but the remainder of her confession was forever lost, surrendered to the final exhalation that signalled her passing.

Thomas's tears flowed again, his despair overwhelming. In his anguished lamentations, a five-year-old girl with golden curls tiptoed into her mother's chamber. Upon beholding her father enshrouded in tears, she cried, "Mama?" understanding the reason behind her Papa's tears.

Aware of the impact such a sight would have on his young daughter, Thomas gently scooped her up into his arms, shielding his precious Jane from the heart-wrenching view of her lifeless mother, an indelible mark that would have marred her tender heart. He carried her to the nursery, where her three younger sisters awaited. Catherine, a newborn, and one-year-old Mary slumbered peacefully in their cribs while three-year-old Elizabeth played happily with her doll, blissfully ignorant of losing her Mama.

Thomas pondered the grave inquiry that weighed heavily upon his bereaved heart. How was he to replace the irreplaceable, motherly figure of the woman who would soon be reduced to dust in the cold earth of a cemetery?

He cursed the cruel fate bestowed upon his beloved daughters, his thoughts promptly turning to the vow he had made to his departed wife. Therefore, he quickly resolved to seek a woman who would fill the void of Jannie's demise. He would give his girls a new mother who would offer them solace and affection.

# Chapter 1

T homas Bennet peered wistfully through the window of his opulent library that held strong evidence of his passion for books; the walls were adorned with a vast collection of weathered volumes, defining the owner's enthusiasm for the written word, with nary a tome left unread. His gaze followed the graceful figures of his two daughters, Jane and Catherine, their captivating looks mirroring the image of their late mother. Sighing deeply, the man found himself reminiscing about the woman who had given him four excellent daughters—she would undoubtedly have been proud of how the girls had grown into beautiful young ladies.

Mr Bennet observed the girls as they meandered amidst the freshly manicured garden, their lively conversation enlivening the air, when a firm knock upon the door jolted him out of his reverie.

He wearily turned to face his wife, bracing himself for another tiresome lecture.

"Mr Bennet, Lizzy and I have just consulted with Hill the issue with the Smiths on the north farm and it should be resolved in a matter of days." With a slight pause, Mrs Bennet continued, "A couple of social obligations require your attention. Tomorrow evening, we are expected to dine with the Gouldings.

Furthermore, we have a new neighbour moving into Netherfield Park."

"Is that so?" He arched a quizzical brow, a flicker of surprise dancing within his green eyes.

"I implore you to pay him a courtesy call," his wife interjected, preempting any objections that may have risen. "I understand your aversion to such social formalities, but it is a mere trifle obligation you must fulfil. Who knows, the gentleman may even extend an invitation to join him for a spot of shooting."

With these instructions, the woman left the room without a second glance at her slothful husband.

Mrs Camila Bennet, née Asher, presented a look that belied her years. Though she had reached the threshold of nine and thirty, an age had bestowed upon her a certain grace, and her countenance, though slightly pale and severe, possessed a dignity that commanded attention.

Upon her union with Mr Bennet, Camila had found herself embracing a role that exceeded mere matrimony. At that time, her stepdaughter Catherine had counted a mere six months, while the eldest girl, Jane, had just celebrated her sixth birthday. Remarkably, her new husband's four daughters embraced Camila as their new mother figure with open hearts, their affections swiftly and seamlessly weaving themselves into the fabric of familial unity. In turn, the woman's affection for the four girls had grown with each passing day, her entire being devoted to filling the void left by the untimely passing of Jannie Bennet.

Indeed, the arrival of the new Mrs Bennet had proved an admirable addition to the family, her disposition assuming an air of dignified severity, attaching great importance to the hallowed principles of propriety.

As she glided into the parlour, Camila paused to cast her discerning gaze upon her daughters, a serene smile gracing her lips. The young ladies were presenting an enchanting picture, each possessing their own distinct charms.

Jane, the eldest at two and twenty, hovered perilously close to the spinsterhood, yet her beauty remained unmatched within the district's confines. Her countenance exuded a tranquillity of spirit and a disposition suffused with sweetness. If Jane could be faulted for anything, it lay in her undying inclination to believe in the inherent goodness of all souls. Such propensity often invited both admiration and vulnerability.

Elizabeth, younger by two years, possessed a countenance that could captivate with its striking green eyes, which flickered with an intelligent spark. Her demeanour, possessed of a playful mien, served as a counterweight to Jane's optimistic tendencies, ensuring a reasonable balance between the sisters.

Mary, the third girl, could not boast of exceptional physical beauty, unlike her elder sisters, for she had weathered a childhood marred by infirmity and frailty. Her eyes, weakened by her past tribulations, bore a certain vulnerability. Yet, in the parlance of the discerning observer, Mary's sober and studious nature commanded respect and intimidated many, for she was the epitome of unwavering diligence.

As for Catherine, she revelled in the heady novelty of her coming out, her youthful exuberance serving as a delightful facade that veiled her malleability.

And then there was Lydia, Mrs Bennet's flesh and blood, clad in the modest attire befitting a girl of fourteen who exhibited the same lively disposition as Elizabeth.

As Camila contemplated her beloved daughters, a profound sense of pride swelled within her breast. Truly, it was a family that any woman would be honoured to call her own.

Following their longstanding custom, the Bennet family had ventured into the south parlour to partake in the afternoon tea.

Having barely settled herself, Lydia could no longer suppress the persistent query plaguing her all morning.

"Pray, do you suppose the gentleman who has chosen to grace Netherfield with his presence shall prove to be amiable? I earnestly hope so! For far too long, we have endured a dearth of neighbours on that particular side."

In her usual amiable tone, Jane replied, "Indeed, it would be quite pleasant if our new neighbour were inclined to attend to the outer fields. Lizzy mentioned that the land adjacent to our sheep pasture was nothing short of a wilderness." With her work-basket in hand, she delicately withdrew the gown she was crafting, holding it aloft to examine her handiwork under the golden streams of sunlight cascading through the windows.

Catherine nodded in agreement. "Undoubtedly, Papa would welcome the company of another neighbour with whom he could engage in hunting and friendly visits. I dare say Papa does not hold Sir William in high regard, in spite of his amiable disposition." Contemplating her own work basket, she inquired, "Jane, may I be of assistance? You shall appear as a perfect angel at the forthcoming assembly."

"Thank you, Kitty," Jane serenely replied, bestowing upon her sister a gentle smile. "Have you not procured a new gown for the dances?"

"Indeed I have," rejoined she, gracefully positioning herself beside her elder sister. "You have marked your hem; shall I commence from there?"

Jane held up the gown in question. "What say you, dear sisters? Should the sleeves be of considerable length or truncated? Aunt Gardiner's latest edition of Harper's magazine suggests that both styles are en vogue this season."

Lydia tilted her head to one side. "Opt for longer sleeves, Jane. The hue of that fawn fabric will undoubtedly illuminate your entire countenance, and with a dainty lace trimming, your delicate hands shall be showcased to great advantage." She retrieved her own basket and placed her lace pillow atop her lap. "I believe I possess ample material in this pattern for your hem. It is an imitation of the latest fashion." Unravelling her lace bobbins with caution, she arranged them neatly in her lap, ensuring not a single thread tangled. "Mary, would you be so kind as to play for us? The light in the room appears sufficient to spare your eyes any strain."

Mary settled herself at the pianoforte situated in the heart of the parlour to maximize the natural light it received throughout the day. "Pray, what piece would you like me to perform?"

"Ah, anything you like! Your musicianship never fails to delight," remarked Lydia.

Lizzy smiled mischievously, a glimmer of amusement dancing in her eyes. "Take care with such requests, Lydia. Mary might deem it appropriate to regale us with a rendition of scales."

Laughter erupted from the sisters as the youngest girl protested, "But even scales would sound melodious when played by Mary!"

Elizabeth leaned over her own basket and retrieved a sizeable, wrapped package. "I had intended to present this to you to-morrow, Mary, but if you are to perform for us, it may as well be offered in advance." She handed the parcel to her sister. "It is a compendium of Mr Beethoven's most recent compositions."

"Oh, Lizzy!" gasped Mary. "I am most grateful!" She blinked rapidly as she meticulously unwrapped the parcel, setting aside the wrapping paper for future use. "Might you join me in one of the duets? Surely there must be several."

"Certainly." Elizabeth seated herself beside Mary at the pianoforte. "Though I fear my own modest skills may mar the beauty of your playing."

"Modesty is a virtue, Lizzy, but one should not disparage oneself unnecessarily," remarked Mrs Bennet, her needle deftly piercing the verdant fabric of the dress she was altering with nimble, precise stitches.

Elizabeth smiled in response, gracefully bowing her head as

she positioned her fingers on the piano keys.

The room was soon filled with the elegant melodies of Beethoven, skilfully played by Mary, while Lizzy accompanied her sister with a gentle harmony. The music swirled through the air, casting a spell of enchantment upon the gathered Bennet sisters.

As the notes resonated, time seemed to pause, capturing the beauty of the moment. Each sister, absorbed in her own task, felt a deep connection to the others, bound by their shared affection and sisterly love. Their spirits truly thrived in these moments of harmony, both musical and familial.

Outside, the gentle breeze whispered through the blossoming trees, casting a dappled pattern of shadows on the lush greenery. The fresh air of late summer wafted through the open windows, infusing the room with a delicate fragrance that mingled with the strains of music.

*∧*∧*

The morrow arrived, and with the breaking of their fast, Elizabeth adorned herself in her well-worn riding attire, embarking upon her customary weekly exploration of the estate. She chose her faithful companion, Blackberry, a gentle mare raised and trained under her careful tutelage from a tender foal. The persistence of youthful trepidation towards equestrian pursuits had not deterred Mrs Bennet from ensuring that her daughters acquired the riding skills befitting young ladies of genteel breeding.

The nuances of Longbourn's estate held Elizabeth's undivided attention as she made her leisurely rounds, exhibiting a thoroughness befitting a lady of her standing. The sun cast its golden glow upon the verdant landscape, illuminating her path as she guided Blackberry with a deft hand. Being as familiar with the course as its equestrian companion, the horse serenely traversed the path.

A cluster of sheep grazed together in the verdant fields, their heavy fleece a source of warmth against the damp climate. Nearby, young James Hill stood to watch, his untrained hands clutching a staff as he surveyed the peaceful scene. Though he lacked the wit to train a dog, his gentle nature and sweet-tempered demeanour won the trust of the sheep, allowing him to inspect them for any potential injury or illness.

In spite of his lack of experience, the boy cared for the creatures with unwavering dedication, tending to their every need and ensuring their well-being in the damp climate.

While inspecting the flock, Elizabeth signalled Blackberry towards the grazing sheep. But before she could take more than a few steps, the sound of gunfire shattered the peaceful air. Blackberry, startled, reared up and pranced nervously while the woman's heart raced with fear as she saw the panicked sheep scattered in all directions, heading straight towards young Hill, who stood frozen with terror.

With no time to waste, Lizzy urged Blackberry into a gallop; her eyes fixed firmly on the sheep and their hapless shepherd. She leaned low in the saddle, guiding the mare with a steady hand as they raced towards the narrowing gap between the sheep and their terrified guardian.

As they closed in on their target, Elizabeth's heart pounded with a rush, her senses honed for the task at hand. With a skill born of years of experience, she deftly steered Blackberry into the path of the fleeing sheep, forcing them to veer away from the hapless young Hill. At that moment, her courage and quick thinking ensured that Longbourn's precious flock remained safe and sound.

The hooves of the noble steed resonated with a resounding thud upon the earth while a melange of fragrances, encompassing the essence of equine, soil, and dishevelled grass, swirled in harmonious union with the less savoury scent of sheep. She manoeuvred past the apprehensive creatures and the youthful Hill, so close that the hem of her riding habit nearly brushed against his countenance. The offside offered no further space, and the bleating animals expressed their panicked state, striving to flee into the embrace of their equally terror-stricken companions.

Elizabeth deftly guided Blackberry, executing a skilful turn, and propelled her gallantly towards the herd once more. This time, the congregation of woolly creatures scattered before her, hastening toward the southern fence in a flurry of motion.

Her heart thumped within her breast as she gradually decelerated the pace of her trusty steed. "Master Hill, are you unharmed?"

The son of Longbourn's housekeeper shook himself vigorously. "Nay, Miss Lizzy. Pray, did this cause harm to the sheep?"

She almost erupted into laughter. How characteristic of young Hill to exhibit greater concern for his woolly charges than for his own well-being!

"No, Master Hill. They ought to be quite unharmed." She cast a withering glare in the direction of the hedgerow demarcating the boundary between Longbourn and Netherfield. "Unless some foolish soul deems it fit to engage in shooting once more."

Only then did Elizabeth perceive the presence of two gentlemen observing from the opposite side of the hedge. Her cheeks flushed at the realisation that they might have overheard her remark. Urging Blackberry closer to the fence, she scrutinised the strangers with measured composure.

The taller figure possessed a darker countenance, evoking a more austere demeanour compared to his fair-haired companion. She conceded that both gentlemen displayed well-proportioned physiques, exuding an air of handsomeness as they sat atop their noble steeds. It seemed that her arrival had amused them, judging by the glint in the eyes of the darker man and the smile adorning the fair one's visage.

Elizabeth Bennet found herself in a most vexatious situation indeed. As she drew near a hedge, she spoke in a measured tone for fear of disturbing the coolness of the surrounding fields.

"Good sirs, I do hope your hunt was successful, though it seems to have come at a high cost to your neighbours, for one of our men was nearly injured." The astonishment that engulfed both men's countenances only fueled her ire. "Did it never occur to you that there might be expansive fields beyond your diminutive wilderness? Surely, men of distinction such as yourselves would not presume to engage in such hunting activities within such cramped confines."

While his friend looked quite crestfallen, a flush of colour rose in the cheeks of the darker gentleman as he uttered, "I beg your pardon, Miss...?"

"Bennet. Elizabeth Bennet," she replied curtly, for she was in no mood for pleasantries. "My father is the owner of those grounds, and he would greatly appreciate it if you would give him notice before engaging in such dangerous pursuits in the future."

The fair-haired gentleman's face took on the hue of his scarlet cravat as he apologised profusely. "I am truly sorry, Miss Bennet. I have recently taken possession of Netherfield Park, and I fear that my exuberance got the better of me."

Elizabeth arched an eyebrow, for she had heard that the estate was quite impressive. "No blame attaches to you, sir," she said with a hint of benevolence. "However, it must be said that the outer fields of Netherfield Park appear somewhat neglected and have the appearance of hunting grounds."

The fair-haired gentleman seemed even more abashed and muttered something about it being entirely his fault.

"This is my friend, Fitzwilliam Darcy," he added after a moment.

Elizabeth bowed in the saddle, acknowledging the

introduction. "The pleasure is mine, sir," she said, her tone now softened.

Mr Darcy returned her bow, but his manner was decidedly distant, and Lizzy could have sworn his ears were suffused with a rosy hue.

"My companion endeavoured to persuade me that this was not the optimal venue for shooting, but I was steadfast in my resolve," declared the fair-haired gentleman and bowed with gallantry. "Charles Bingley, at your service, madam."

Elizabeth responded with dignified courtesy.

By that time, Mr Darcy must have composed himself enough to speak with propriety, for he inquired, "Your servant, Miss Bennet? Has he been harmed?"

At least both gentlemen displayed a certain level of decorum, Elizabeth mused. "Master Hill is in good health, sir. I appreciate your concern." She turned to follow Mr Darcy's gaze and exhaled when she observed Hill meticulously inspecting each sheep, ensuring their well-being.

"Pardon me, Miss Bennet, but I must express my surprise at the sight of these sheep. Might I inquire..." Mr Bingley's voice trailed off as he realised the impropriety of such a query addressed to a lady.

The woman met his gaze unflinchingly. "They are merino sheep, imported from Spain, Mr Bingley. We hold them in high regard here at Longbourn."

Darcy's countenance grew sterner, his blush fading away.

"Perhaps you could converse with Mr Bennet at your convenience, Mr Bingley?" suggested she. "My father may possess more knowledge about the management of Netherfield than your representative has imparted." Trifles such as the location of the hunting fields, she mused.

"Capital!" cried Mr Bingley, his smile returning. "I must say Longbourn appears to be an admirable estate, a testament to Mr Bennet's credit, I am sure."

"Thank you, Mr Bingley," said she, and added, "If your hunting pursuits are not yet sated, pray make use of the vast field southwards which adjoins Sir William's and our own estate's hunting grounds. An agreement was settled upon some time ago to ensure that all three lands had ample space for game." A mischievous sprite within her being prompted her to add, "Perhaps it would be prudent to pay a visit to Sir William just to ascertain that he does not intend to roam the fields during your own excursion?"

Mr Darcy's lips twitched with amusement, though his countenance remained sombre. His companion, meanwhile, beamed at her and replied, "Well spoken, Miss Bennet. I am certain we shall all be excellent neighbours."

But before she could utter a farewell, young Hill's cry for aid jolted her from the company's tiresome chatter. "Miss Lizzy! I do believe the old ewe is lambing!"

"Excuse me, gentlemen," said she briskly, her haste compelling her to take swift action. "I fear I have an urgent matter to attend to." Raising her voice, she called out, "Hill, I shall join you directly."

Without wasting more time, she dismounted from her horse, deftly securing the reins to the hedgerow. She gathered her skirts and prepared to assist the poor ewe in her distress when she heard Mr Darcy's voice, clear as a bell.

"Goodness, Bingley! What were you thinking, encouraging such shrewish behaviour?"

A shrew, Mr Darcy? Elizabeth's thoughts raced with indignation. We shall see about that!

# Chapter 2

Temptation and Mr Fitzwilliam Darcy were hardly unfamiliar acquaintances. Indeed, the man's association with allurement had been both protracted and decidedly ungenial. Since his father's untimely demise during his own tender years, Darcy had shouldered the weighty responsibilities of managing the vast Pemberley estate while ensuring that his considerably younger sister, Georgiana, received an education and upbringing befitting her station and disposition.

With her dear mother long since departed from this earthly realm and then bereaved of her beloved father, Miss Darcy naturally looked to her brother as both guardian and guide. Therefore, while his peers had been chasing the affections of young maidens—wont to frolic and gallivant—and striving to avoid the pitfalls of hasty matrimony, Darcy had been performing his duties diligently in spite of his still tender age.

And while he did not find discontent in the trajectory of his life, there were occasions when the weight of his obligations chafed against his sensibilities. Even this present visit to his amiable friend served as both a gratification and a chore, for it entailed his perpetual guidance in matters pertaining to the management of a grand establishment.

Darcy did not anticipate Bingley to devolve into a parasitic creature, exploiting his tenantry and lands only to rail bitterly against their perceived inadequacies. However, the constant requests for counsel on sundry affairs weighed upon him, a demand that he, bound by the dictates of honour, could not lightly disregard.

And yet, none of these circumstances adequately elucidated why Darcy found himself utterly unable to disentangle his thoughts from the impropriety of a genteel young lady comporting herself as though she were the progeny of the very landowner she inhabited.

Miss Elizabeth Bennet had exhibited a remarkable display of horsemanship and courage that could rival any gentleman's when she expertly herded those hapless sheep away from the simple-minded boy tasked with tending them. Such a feat was entirely admirable, yet her subsequent conduct was less so.

The gentleman's countenance burned with shame at the recollection of her rebuke, which was doubly humiliating, as it was rightfully deserved. He ought to have prevented Bingley from engaging in shooting within such a confined space. However, to have a lady chastise him in such a manner was intolerable. The proper management of an estate was a task reserved for men, and surely, if Mr Bennet was not able to oversee the estate himself, other capable individuals should assume the responsibility.

"Come, Darcy, I am sure you have not listened to a word I have uttered," declared Bingley, his usual amiable and genial tone resonating throughout the countryside.

Darcy arched one eyebrow. "I presume that the praise of one field is akin to any other."

Bingley's cheeks flushed with embarrassment. "I beg your pardon, Darcy. Netherfield Park is simply ideal for my current situation, and I forget that you have been managing Pemberley for several years now."

"My apologies," replied his companion. "The peculiarity of your neighbour's circumstances has been weighing heavily on my mind."

"And not the comely countenance of the young lady?" Bingley's grin lacked any malicious intent. "It would not be an embarrassment for even you, Darcy, to find her captivating."

"Heaven forbid," declared Darcy, shaking his head and nudging his steed closer to his friend. "Surely, you found it strange for a young lady to be performing such duties."

"Indeed," Bingley concurred. "But, Darcy, she may not possess a choice in the matter."

In response to Darcy's inquisitive gaze, his friend elucidated, "The estate agent informed me that I might encounter difficulties securing capable staff for Netherfield Park. The toll of war is evident, of course, but when Lord Altmont made an advantageous match, most of the seasoned workers flocked to Somerford Hall hoping to secure employment there and never returned." Bingley gestured in a manner that conveyed his helplessness. "This explains the scarcity of male labourers in this vicinity."

Darcy, to his dismay, realised that he had failed to observe the evident truth. In spite of priding himself on his keen discernment, he had failed to recognise the deplorable absence of mature gentlemen. Netherfield's servants and tenants boasted an abundance of the old and young, but the number of mature men amongst the tenants was far fewer than he had anticipated and scarce among the servants as well. "You are correct," he forced a smile, conceding his oversight. "I should have been more attentive."

If only Miss Bennet's angered gaze, with its fleeting glimmer of amusement as she had teased him about the hunting fields, would cease tormenting him! He could not associate himself with a lady of such disposition. Even if she were an heiress, she should not possess knowledge of matters as mundane as sheep breeds, let alone have the audacity to counsel a gentleman on such affairs.

Yet, the composure with which she had responded to the

simple-minded shepherd's lament regarding a ewe's lambing, the courage she had exhibited in rushing to aid the boy, and the kindness she had extended to him, were all admirable. Darcy reluctantly acknowledged that had Mr Bennet's son acted in a similar manner, he would have been genuinely impressed and more than willing to offer assistance in any necessary endeavour.

An unsettling suspicion gnawed at him. Miss Bennet would not likely view his reasoning kindly, and worse still, she would undoubtedly highlight every flaw that had eluded his perception, employing the impeccable manners she had so flawlessly exhibited. Had such a perplexing contradiction ever existed in a single, slender female?

"If my memory serves me right," Bingley interjected, "Miss Elizabeth Bennet is one of five Miss Bennets. The four other young ladies are reputed to be exquisite beauties, though the youngest has yet to make her debut."

Darcy nodded in agreement. "If they all possess the charms of Miss Elizabeth Bennet, they would undoubtedly be regarded as beauties in any gathering."

Not that she conformed to the standards of classical beauty. Her countenance possessed a strength that defied such notions, yet her expressive eyes and self-assured demeanour overshadowed any imperfections. As for her figure, if there were any flaws, he had yet to perceive them.

Bingley chuckled. "Ah, so she did catch your attention!" He playfully doffed his hat in a mock bow. "I must say, my friend, I am duly impressed. But fret not, for Miss Bennets do not frequent the lofty realms that you inhabit."

This time, Darcy arched both his eyebrows in surprise.

"The estate's agent does tend to be rather loquacious," Bingley confessed. "One might even say gossipy, were he of the fairer sex." His grin widened. "I fear I shall never recall all the information he imparted to me. I can only hope to retain the essential advice to spare myself from disaster."

"A sentiment shared by us all." Darcy's voice caught in his throat. The catastrophe that had nearly befallen his dearest sister clouded any semblance of pleasure that might attempt to ensnare him.

Yet, the recollection of Miss Bennet did more than merely tempt him. Even knowing that she was surely beneath his station, he found himself entangled in the conundrum of admiration and consternation. Her actions during that brief encounter had been remarkably commendable, yet the impropriety of a gentleman's daughter assuming the role of her father's... She must be aware that her actions would mark her, at best, as a shrew and, at worst, as a hoyden.

In spite of his resolute determination to banish thoughts of Miss Elizabeth Bennet from his mind, Darcy found himself unable to resist the constant pull, each recollection yielding further aspects to both admire and lament. If this were to be the recurring pattern of his stay at Netherfield, it would be prudent for him to devise a pretext to return to the sanctity of Pemberley and swiftly at that.

*∧*∧*

Elizabeth's composure was not fully restored until she had returned to the comfortable confines of Longbourn and exchanged her attire for a modest day dress fashioned from sprigged linen. The encounter with her new neighbour and his companion had already rattled her sensibilities, but the unfortunate incident involving James Hill had pushed her into further disarray. In that unfortunate moment, when the ewe had chosen to bring forth new life, Lizzy was confronted with a discomfiting and disagreeable spectacle.

The truth of the matter was that Elizabeth had long recognised the discomfort and messiness inherent in the birthing process, a revelation far removed from the idyllic descriptions she had encountered in her readings on animal husbandry. Yet, she had not dared to lend her direct assistance, opting instead to provide encouragement to young Hill while shielding herself from the distressing sight. The young boy's state of bewilderment demanded her attention, and she had resolved to keep her gaze averted, refusing to subject herself to the additional horrors lurking within an animal's labour. Yet, she could not have helped but see a glimpse of the whole process, and she feared it would stay with her for a long time.

Once she had attired herself suitably and arranged her chestnut curls, Elizabeth made her way to the dining room, where two maids were busily laying out luncheon dishes. Lizzy beckoned one of them and requested her presence in the still room at her earliest convenience.

The still room exuded a calm, dry ambience, permeated with a melange of aromas emanating from the drying and dried herbs. Lavender bundles dangled from the ceiling while wooden receptacles for desiccated herbs adorned the shelves. Lizzy had spent many a delightful hour here with Jane, securing bundles of cut herbs to be hung for drying. Yet, in recent days, she had found herself in the company of Lydia, imparting the knowledge of which herbs held the most benefit for specific purposes whilst fielding an endless barrage of inquiries regarding her own social debut and the potentiality of eligible young gentlemen within the vicinity.

The girl was all too aware of the lack of suitable suitors within the Meryton district, a dire circumstance which had severely limited her chances of securing a favourable match.

Sir William's eldest son was a mere thirteen years of age, and both the Bennet and Lucas families had long been considered the most genteel of the district's inhabitants. In spite of his honourable title, Sir William's circumstances were similar to those of the Bennets, and therefore, neither Charlotte nor Maria, his two daughters, had the privilege of partaking in a

London season. The only other families worthy of social calls were those of affluent tradesmen, such as attorneys and the like. Even there, the allure of military life and the potential for advancement enticed many of these families' sons to venture far from the district. The allure of military life and the potential for advancement that an officer's career might afford had led many of the district's young men to seek their fortunes elsewhere, leaving behind a dearth of suitable suitors for the local ladies.

In the midst of their conversation, the arrival of the housekeeper caused them to break their chatter. "Miss Lizzy! Pray tell, is my James safe and sound?" inquired Mrs Hill, her apron in a flurry.

Elizabeth hastened to soothe her anxieties. "Yes, Hill, your son is quite well. However, he did have quite a fright. If he returns home with bloodied clothing, it is only from the lamb that made its appearance today."

"A lamb, Miss Lizzy? Our James tended to a lamb?" cried the woman, her hands unclenching from her apron in amazement.

"Indeed, a strong and healthy lamb. When last I saw it, the little creature was already standing on its own four feet," she replied with a gentle smile. "Though I fear the excitement of it may cause your son to forget the messiness of the birthing process and the fright he had experienced when the sheep were startled by the nearby shots fired from Netherfield Park's adjoining field."

Elizabeth recounted the details of the incident to the housekeeper as was appropriate, emphasising that the boy had suffered no more than a fright. His mother lifted one hand to her mouth, then slowly lowered it as Lizzy put her fears to rest.

"Thank you, Miss Lizzy," said she, relieved. "You have been so kind to our boy. Not many would take such care with a half-wit."

"James is a skilled hand with the sheep, Hill," Elizabeth reminded her with a smile. "They trust him completely, and so long as nothing startles him, he cares for them with the utmost diligence. I have already requested the cowherds to check on him this afternoon to ensure he has settled, so there should be no further concerns aside from the need for laundering - or perhaps even replacing - his shirt."

Mrs Hill's countenance eased, and she attempted a tentative smile. "Thank you, Miss Lizzy. I shall make certain that James is thoroughly cleaned up and properly attired for tomorrow's pursuits."

Once the woman departed, reassured of her youngest child's well-being, Elizabeth selected one of the bundles of dried lavender to infuse her homemade trunk freshener with a delightful fragrance. She looked forward to indulging in the period before dinner, basking in the company of her sisters.

*∧*∧*

"Oh, dear Lizzy! Have you tarnished your standing with the gentlemen?" inquired Kitty with a sympathetic tone.

Elizabeth merely chuckled. During pleasant afternoons, the ladies of Longbourn embarked on leisurely strolls to various picturesque spots within their vicinity. Engaging in such exercise was beneficial for their physical well-being. It adhered to Mrs Bennet's insistence that they walk no less than two miles each day, weather permitting, thereby ensuring that they maintained the epitome of good health.

"Considering the spectacle I made of myself by assuming a man's role, I highly doubt I possess any standing among the gentlemen," Elizabeth reassured her sister, a playful glint in her eye. "It shall be left to Jane, Mary, or you to captivate their hearts."

"Lizzy!" protested both Mary and Jane in unison.

"If these gentlemen are foolish enough to overlook your charms, then Lydia's entrance into society will undoubtedly quell their resistance," she replied confidently.

Catherine shook her head. "Oh, no! Do you truly intend for Lydia and me to wed such fine gentlemen when you, Jane, and Mary possess far greater accomplishments than we?"

Mrs Bennet emitted a soft clucking sound. "Kitty, you are just as accomplished as your sisters. It is unfortunate that Lizzy was observed handling estate affairs, but her involvement was a necessary evil. I believe it is not an impression that cannot be rectified through proper conduct when in the company of gentlemen at the assembly."

"Oh, but you did not witness their countenances, Mama," remarked Elizabeth, gracefully brushing aside a young oak branch that extended across their path and holding it so that her sisters might pass unhindered. "I can scarcely imagine a worse situation unless I were to don Papa's attire and converse like a man."

At Mrs Bennet's gasp of horror, Lizzy added, "These gentlemen are of the highest calibre, undoubtedly unaccustomed to young ladies being thrust into unbecoming circumstances due to unfortunate events."

Laughter filled the air, emanating from all her sisters, though Jane interjected, "Lizzy, you ought not to jest so. The gentlemen may have simply been taken aback."

"Jane speaks with wisdom," Camila Bennet pronounced, her judgment forever impeccable. "One should refrain from drawing hasty conclusions based on such scant evidence, Lizzy."

Elizabeth lowered her head in acknowledgement of Mrs Bennet's point. "Do not fret, Mama. I shall henceforth be the epitome of ladylike virtue." She nimbly leapt over a fallen branch. "After all, I, too, must secure a husband who is willing to accept me in spite of my modest possessions." She turned to assist Mary, who, unlike her sturdy sisters, often stumbled on uneven paths due to her delicate constitution.

"Silly!" cried Lydia, her smile radiant. "You possess the same accomplishments as Jane, Mary, and Kitty."

They emerged from the woods, arriving near the imposing gates of Longbourn, and proceeded to stroll along the estate's extensive driveway. Elizabeth's breath caught in her throat upon glimpsing two mounted horsemen dismounting near the entrance.

"Goodness me!" whispered Kitty. "Could those be the gentlemen you encountered, Lizzy?"

Elizabeth nodded, startled by their unexpected appearance at Longbourn.

"They are truly distinguished gentlemen," stated Kitty quietly.

On this point, Elizabeth held no doubt. The bay geldings upon which the men rode were magnificent creatures, obediently yielding to the reins held by the grooms. As she had observed that very morning, the men themselves were as handsome as any lady could wish, attired in fashionable garments that embraced the latest trends without indulging in excess. She found herself instinctively reaching up to adjust her bonnet but quickly suppressed the urge with a touch of irritation. She would not indulge in primping or preening before these gentlemen, regardless of their undeniable elegance!

It appeared that the sisters' approach had not gone unnoticed by the gentlemen as their conversation abruptly ceased. Both men turned their gaze, and Mr Darcy's eyes widened with what seemed like astonishment.

His countenance first paled, then flushed crimson. Fixing his gaze upon Mary, he demanded, "What on earth brings you here? Your mother would never condone such a venture!"

The surprised eruption of Mr Darcy's extraordinary outburst left Elizabeth in a state of speechlessness, rendering her momentarily incapable of uttering a single word. Fortunately for her unwavering determination to project the very embodiment of refined feminine virtue in the presence of these gentlemen, it was Mary who regained her vocal faculties first.

"I humbly beg your pardon, sir," uttered she tenderly, the sweetness of her tone surpassing the most sanguine expectations. "I must confess that you possess an advantage over me in this perplexing situation."

The man, taken aback, found himself growing even more crimson as if his cheeks were set ablaze by an invisible fire. After a brief pause, he executed a curt bow. "I offer my sincerest apologies, madam. Your countenance bears an uncanny resemblance to—" he hesitated, "to a lady whom I am intimately acquainted with." He swallowed hard, his countenance suddenly fixated upon the gravel beneath his feet as though seeking solace in its meagre presence. "Regrettably, I have inadvertently lapsed into improper discourse, startled as I was by your resemblance to said lady."

Mary, in response, replied with a demure curtsy and an enchanting smile that assuredly eluded Darcy's sight, for his gaze remained resolutely affixed to the ground. "All is forgiven, sir. One can readily empathise with the disconcerting experience of unexpectedly encountering an individual whom one presumed to be far removed, preoccupied with other endeavours, in a place such as this." Not a trace of mirth could be detected in her voice, though Elizabeth discerned a glimmer of mischief dancing within her sister's brown eyes.

Visibly startled, Darcy looked up, though his perturbation persisted undeniably etched upon his countenance. "Your generosity knows no bounds, Madam."

Elizabeth chided herself, urging reason to prevail. The gentleman had undoubtedly been subjected to a great disturbance, and his profound embarrassment justified his somewhat curt demeanour.

Mrs Bennet intervened with her customary politeness and excellent manners. "Gentlemen, I shall inform my husband, Mr Bennet, of your arrival."

Darcy's gaze remained fixed upon the floor as a servant

guided him and Bingley through the halls of Longbourn, leading them to the library. By avoiding any direct eye contact, he sought to shield himself from the weight of his own humiliation.

It was grievous enough that he had mistakenly taken one of Miss Bennets for his own cousin, but to have carelessly blurted out such a demand in the face of the alarming possibility of his aunt's arrival in this tranquil corner of Hertfordshire was truly inexcusable. Moreover, his lack of propriety could tarnish Bingley's standing amongst the young ladies. While they may be of a lower social station, the daughters of a modest country gentleman presented a suitable prospect for his amiable friend to consider.

Indeed, the Bennet family held no significant distinction, for had they been of consequence, he would have surely encountered them during his numerous visits to London throughout the seasons. Darcy was confident that he had never laid eyes upon any of the young ladies before this very day. And he would certainly have noticed a young lady possessing Miss Elizabeth Bennet's striking green eyes or one who bore a resemblance to his own cousin.

It was unlikely that the young ladies had shunned London due to their inferior appearance, as even the youngest, attired in plain and modest dresses befitting a young girl not yet introduced to society, surpassed the beauty of many self-proclaimed belles. The lady he had mistakenly identified as his cousin may have been the least captivating of the sisters, yet when separated from their company, she would undoubtedly radiate her own charm. Just as a primrose, though unable to contend with the ostentatious splendour of a rose, possessed its own loveliness when not overshadowed.

Therefore, either their birth was inferior, or their means were limited. Darcy suspected the latter, as he observed no distinguishing signs of affluence in the surroundings of Longbourn. There were other indications of frugality as well, such as a maid escorting him and Bingley rather than a manservant—a detail that swiftly led Darcy to regard Mr Bennet as a gentleman of minor consequence burdened by financial constraints during their brief journey to the library.

Upon reaching their destination, the gentlemen were warmly received by the master of the house. Darcy estimated the man to be in his late forties at least, his countenance having transitioned from handsome in his youth to a somewhat avuncular figure with first greying hair and spectacles.

After the necessary introductions were made, Mr Bennet invited them to be seated and offered them a glass of port. Though of exceptional quality, the crystal vessels displayed signs of frequent use and adhered to a style that had long fallen out of fashion.

A few pleasant remarks were exchanged concerning the excellent weather as well as Bingley's favourable impression of Netherfield—naturally, a sentiment that found ready agreement. Yet, Mr Bennet eventually remarked, "While your visit is certainly flattering, gentlemen, I highly doubt that such esteemed company would grace my home merely out of neighbourly courtesy."

"Indeed, you are correct, sir," Bingley leaned forward and admitted. "We have come—well, it is I alone who bears the blame —to offer our apologies for startling your sheep this morning. If Miss Elizabeth had not been present, they might have caused harm to your shepherd."

"Who, I assure you, is as scatter-brained as the very creatures he tends," interjected Bennet with a knowing tone. "I must implore you to understand that he is the best we could procure for the task."

"Indeed, we have heard that skilled hands are in great demand in this area," Bingley concurred. "How dire is the situation, truly? I fear that while Netherfield's agent was quite talkative, not all of his information proved particularly useful."

A smile adorned Bennet's countenance once more, exuding

his customary affable charm. "Ah, you mean he tends to engage in idle gossip? Fear not. My Lizzy possesses a wealth of knowledge and shall provide you with any pertinent information you may require."

Try as he might, Mr Darcy could not suppress his astonishment. Surely, Bennet would not openly acknowledge his daughter's unfavourable circumstances?

The older man heaved a heavy sigh, reclining further into his chair. "I know I should not burden her with such responsibilities, but who else is there?" He shook his head ruefully. "There is not a man worthy of entrusting with an estate for miles around. My wife is preoccupied with raising and chaperoning our daughters, running a house and taking care of the tenants. And unfortunately, I myself am ill-suited to the task."

Bingley, as expected, accepted Bennet's words at face value.

Darcy, however, discerned a trace of irony in the gentleman's words—a subtle suggestion that Mr Bennet did not entirely disapprove of his daughter assuming a role traditionally reserved for men.

Bennet's gaze sharpened, betraying a shrewdness that belied his genial appearance. "Mr Darcy, rest assured that I am well aware of the burdens my Lizzy bears." His hands spread wide in a gesture of resignation. "Suffice it to say, Longbourn is entailed to a distant cousin in the absence of male heirs, and thus any savings my daughters can manage shall prove beneficial when it comes to securing their dowries."

Admitting one's financial troubles so bluntly might be deemed imprudent. Yet, Darcy surmised that the matter was common knowledge in this locality, hence posing no difficulty for Mr Bennet to disclose.

In an effort to alleviate the tension, Bingley leaned forward and requested, "Sir, would you be so kind as to enlighten us further on the subject of your sheep?"

*∧*∧*

Amidst the backdrop of an exceptional dinner, Elizabeth's palate experienced but a mere hint of the delightful repast. She was acutely aware of the presence of their unanticipated guests, Mr Darcy and Mr Bingley, and of the former's penetrating gaze that appeared to meticulously catalogue every aspect of Longbourn's dining room, from the plate to the very wallpaper.

While Mr Bingley exuded charisma and amiability, his companion remained reticent; his utterances imbued with an air of curt disdain as if he found the necessity of conversation disagreeable. Yet, whenever Elizabeth inadvertently stole a glance in his direction, the gentleman's eyes were unmistakably fixated upon her, promptly evading her gaze as if apprehensive of their encounter.

In such circumstances, her determination to embody the epitome of refined feminine comportment was tested to its limits. Her solace, however, emanated from Jane's adept ability to steer the discourse away from perilous subjects whenever it teetered on treacherous ground, as well as the whimsical word games enjoyed by her vivacious younger sisters.

Alas, the equilibrium of the evening was disrupted when Mary, in response to Mr Bingley's effusive praise of Mr Darcy's friendship and sensible counsel, quoted Othello with an ironic twist: "My friend, honest, honest Darcy."

Elizabeth's stomach lurched with genuine queasiness as she retorted, "Indeed, it is most veracious that I have beheld truth askew and strangely."

Lydia's eyes widened with intrigue. "Now, Lizzy, hath our discontented winter transformed into a glorious summer?"

Elizabeth was nearly moved to embrace her sister. "Alas, poor Mary! I was acquainted with her, Lydia."

"Aye, there's the quandary," Catherine chimed in. "To be or

not to be, that is the question."

Darcy arched a single eyebrow. "Is this a sword I perceive before me?" His gaze bore directly into Elizabeth's eyes, causing her cheeks to blush as she averted her gaze.

"Sober virtue, the passage of years, and modesty safeguard my innocence," murmured she. "I fervently pray for clemency."

"Oh, Lizzy!" Kitty shook her head, a smile gracing her handsome countenance. "The quality of mercy is not strained; it falls as gently as the rain from heaven."

"And yet, once more unto the breach," responded Darcy, a flicker of amusement sparkling beneath his austere facade. "For I have beheld the majestic heights of the celestial realm, how resplendent!"

A slight twitch played upon Elizabeth's lips as she mused, even while pondering the peculiar notion that this gentleman had deemed her a shrew. "An upright gentleman," she declared, her head tilting ever so slightly as she regarded him. "And a courteous one, and a kind one, and a handsome one, and, I dare say, a virtuous one."

Darcy offered a slight bow over his plate. "A palpable hit!"

Elizabeth could not help but think that his smile transformed him entirely as she joined the gentleman and her sisters in mirthful laughter. Her mother, in spite of her solemn appearance, allowed a little smile to tug at her lips too.

In this cheerful state, Mr Darcy appeared as an entirely different creature. What could have caused his perpetual ill-humour?

"Allow me to apologise," interjected Elizabeth once the laughter had subsided. "Our penchant for this diversion is a customary indulgence amongst us. It was impolite to ensnare you within its bounds." A touch of mischief danced in her eyes as she bestowed upon him a playful smile. "However, I must admit, you acquitted yourself admirably."

"I find this game both diverting and delightful, Miss

Elizabeth," responded he, his momentary amusement fading as he returned to his chilly and severe demeanour. "Pray, do not cease on my account. The works of the Bard can never be deemed inappropriate, even in their most intriguing moments."

"Would you extend the same sentiment to Homer, Mr Darcy?" interjected Mary, her tone carrying a hint of primness. "Or to Sappho?"

Before Lizzy could intervene and protest Mary's impudent question, a frown etched itself upon Darcy's countenance, his expression darkening ever so slightly. "I would posit that such judgments are contingent upon the lady in question, Miss Mary."

"And what of a lady who has acquainted herself with the knowledge of animal husbandry?" Elizabeth found herself inquiring, unable to resist the temptation.

Darcy cleared his throat, regaining his composure. "Any lady who acquaints herself with such matters and yet retains her dignity and refinement," he nodded towards Elizabeth, a tacit acknowledgement of his perception of her as such, "may peruse even the most scandalous of literary material with a clear conscience. For she possesses the discernment to remain impervious to the perils of Roman or Greek impropriety."

Elizabeth swallowed, and her face ablaze with a mixture of embarrassment and intrigue. She could not ascertain whether the gentleman intended to compliment or slight her. However, she found herself experiencing both sentiments simultaneously, utterly perplexed about how to respond.

The air in the room grew charged with unspoken tension, and her thoughts swirled in a storm of emotions. It was as if a clandestine dance of words had commenced between them, where meanings hid behind delicate phrases, and glances held the weight of unspoken truths.

Finally, breaking the spell, Elizabeth summoned her wit and spoke, her voice tinged with a hint of flirtation. "Sir, you possess a remarkable talent for engaging in lively repartee, a quality that has undoubtedly endeared you to many a discerning soul."

Darcy's demeanour softened imperceptibly, a gleam of appreciation shimmering within his eyes. "I am humbled by your gracious words, Miss Elizabeth. The art of conversation, when graced with your presence, becomes an endeavour of unparalleled pleasure."

Their exchange, although seemingly innocuous to others, carried a subtle undercurrent that whispered of an unspoken connection, a shared understanding that went beyond the confines of conventional civility. At that moment, Lizzy wondered if the perceived animosity between them was, in truth, a masquerade concealing a deeper intrigue.

*∧*∧*

The pale glow of a waxing moon filtered through the windows of Mr Darcy's chamber at Netherfield, casting a dim light upon his restless pacing. When he had acceded to Bingley's request for a sojourn to inspect the youthful gentleman's newly acquired demesne, with the added purpose of evading his sisters' tiresome company, Darcy had anticipated nothing more than an agreeable rural jaunt, albeit tarnished by Miss Caroline Bingley's ceaseless and tedious attempts to ensnare his attentions, abetted by her pliable sister, Mrs Hurst, and her indolent husband.

The avoidance of such company would prove to be an uncomplicated affair when the family arrived to-morrow afternoon, for neither lady, he was sure, would exhibit the slightest inclination to forsake the comforts of Netherfield Park, and Hurst himself would harbour no desire to savour the bucolic air.

However, Darcy had not anticipated the compulsion to partake in the society of a local gentleman, much less one blessed with five daughters whose matrimonial prospects were as scant as their visages were comely. Yet, even that circumstance might not have proved burdensome had it not been for the young ladies themselves. In spite of Miss Elizabeth Bennet's disconcerting behaviour earlier in the day, she had assumed the semblance of exemplary decorum throughout the present evening. However, her remarkable eyes had frequently betrayed the sentiments she sought to conceal. She possessed the capacity to converse with an unassailable composure and wit while her expressive green orbs divulged the depths of her true emotions.

This peculiarity, in itself, would be intriguing yet scarcely perturbing. However, Miss Mary's striking resemblance to his cousin Anne had compelled Darcy into exhibiting lamentable lapses in manners, driven, in no small part, by the apprehension that his aunt, Lady Catherine de Bourgh, had trailed him to Hertfordshire in order to inveigle him into making an offer to Anne.

Though his cousin was a sufficiently amiable lady, her constitution was frail, and she remained wholly under the domination of her formidable mother in spite of her adult age. Since the untimely demise of Sir Lewis de Bourgh, his wife's obstinacy and determination had gone unchecked. Even Darcy's mother's whimsical fancy, which had posited that he and Anne, so proximate in age and kindred, would form an enchanting match, had been ensnared by Lady Catherine's machinations contorted into an inexorable decree. Darcy could recollect only two individuals who had dared to defy his aunt's caprices: his deceased father and Sir Lewis, now consigned to the annals of history. The passage of years devoid of any restraint on her demands had rendered his aunt insufferable and, worse still, fostered the delusion that all things must inevitably bow to her will.

However, in spite of her resemblance to Anne, Miss Mary Bennet bore no resemblance to his cousin's character, or rather, she evoked an uncanny resemblance to what Anne might have become if not plagued by perpetual infirmity and cowed into submission by her mother's dominance. If that were not disquieting enough, some Miss Bennets stirred within him a reminiscence of his family in some measure.

The eldest of the sisters, Miss Bennet, possessed a captivating mannerism of intertwining her delicate fingers whenever she engaged in contemplation, much akin to his aunt's inclination when provoked into deep reflection on any given subject. The graceful gestures of Miss Elizabeth, the pursing of her lips in moments of distress or concern, evoked a striking resemblance to his uncle, the Earl. Whenever Miss Catherine experienced a sudden startle or unease, her instinctive withdrawal mirrored the retreat of Anne from her own mother's presence.

In discreet inquiries made throughout the evening, Darcy had learned that Mrs Bennet had actually been a birth mother only to Miss Lydia, and the rest of the girls had had another mother, Mrs Jannie Bennet, who had passed away shortly after giving birth to Miss Catherine.

Moreover, the late Mrs Bennet had a sister, Mrs Phillips, who resided in Meryton, the neighbouring village, and a much younger brother, Mr Gardiner, a prosperous merchant residing in London. Though any plausible connection appeared far-fetched, conversing with the Bennet sisters imparted an inexplicable familiarity reminiscent of his visits to Rosings on those rare occasions when his aunt displayed a favourable disposition.

Darcy sighed, his head shaking in disbelief. Women who exhibited ill-tempered behaviour, only to transform into paragons of sweetness mere hours later, left a perplexing impression on him. His aunt's mannerisms seemed to haunt his every glance.

And then there was the matter of a gentleman permitting, nay, encouraging his daughter to oversee the management of his estate...

The immediate and profound infatuation of Bingley for the eldest Miss Bennet did not ease matters, Darcy pondered. Not that there was any fault to find in the lady herself, but he could well imagine the response of Bingley's sisters to their brother's enamoured state. Hurst, a well-connected and affluent gentleman, often appeared confounded by his wife, as if the woman he had courted and the one he had wedded were two entirely distinct individuals. Having witnessed the behaviour of Miss Bingley, Darcy could not doubt that Hurst was grappling with precisely such a predicament.

The imminent prospect of condescending encounters at the Meryton Assembly, a mere few days hence, nearly convinced Darcy to truncate his visit and hasten back to the comforts of Pemberley.

Though he harboured a natural aversion to social gatherings, his inherent solemn disposition, coupled with a natural aloofness that proved impossible to conceal, rendered such affairs an ordeal, even among friends. Yet Darcy could not deny a modicum of curiosity. He felt certain that Miss Bennets would render the genteel manners of Miss Bingley and Mrs Hurst insipid and affected while appearing nothing less than perfectly poised and amiable young ladies.

If their presence were to coax the Bingley sisters into hastening their retreat to Hurst's townhouse in London, Darcy would be considerably more inclined to prolong his stay at Netherfield.

Perhaps it was time to dispatch a letter to his cousin, Colonel Fitzwilliam, suggesting his involvement in their present company. He and Bingley shared a tolerable camaraderie, and Fitzwilliam held the same disdain for Bingley's sisters as Darcy himself. Furthermore, his cousin could provide reassurances that Miss Bennets were nothing more than they appeared to be, dispelling any misguided notions arising from Miss Mary's resemblance to Anne.

Yes, that plan would suit admirably, Darcy mused, his gaze fixed upon the moonlit landscape, lost in contemplation. Though unconventional for a gentleman to pen letters under the enchanting glow of the moon, it was indeed a possibility worth entertaining. With a decisive nod, he resolved to proceed.

# Chapter 3

As the hour of the assembly approached, chaos reigned within the Bennet household. With four unmarried daughters to attend, and a bevvy of unattached gentlemen set to attend, the entire family was abuzz with preparations. Given her age, Catherine was the most eligible of Bennet's sisters and was the focus of much attention. Maids fussed over her new gown while her sisters worked to remove any tangles from her hair and style it into the fashionable mass of ringlets that were in vogue.

Lydia deftly intertwined freshly plucked white rosebuds into her sister's dark-blonde locks, utilizing thornless stems as a means of securing the floral arrangement. At the same time, Mary, whose straight and brown locks resisted the allure of curls, opted for a simple coiffure that possessed an ageless elegance.

The Bennet girls collectively bestowed extra care upon their appearance, acutely aware that every young lady of marriageable age within the vicinity would be meticulously primped and adorned, with hopes of capturing the attention of the esteemed Mr Bingley or the enigmatic Mr Darcy.

Elizabeth would have found such prospects rather amusing were it not for Mr Darcy's cold demeanour, which swiftly relegated him to the status of haughty and disagreeable in the eyes of Meryton's matrons. Yet, she remained steadfast in her conviction that the gentleman concealed a far more tender disposition beneath his fastidious politeness. The occasional unguarded moments she managed to catch glimpses of during their encounters hinted at a man who held no great affection for societal gatherings and concealed his discomfort behind a surface that could easily be misconstrued as pride or disagreeability.

Indeed, Lizzy could not bring herself to accept that he warranted the ill-natured gossip circulating among the idle minds of Meryton. Consequently, she and her sisters resolved to rescue him from the shackles of his own disposition, thus preventing the unfavourable impression he left on their insignificant little town from forever poisoning the narrow minds of its inhabitants.

Mrs Bennet, ever supportive of Lizzy's design, joined forces with Mary and Kitty, engaging in lengthy deliberations on how best to disarm Mr Darcy and put him at ease. Jane, though not excluded from their scheming, contributed little, for all the Bennet sisters, save Jane, were convinced that Mr Bingley would claim her company for the evening. As for Lydia, her unseasoned status precluded her from direct action, yet she swore to alert her sisters should she chance upon Mr Darcy trapped by one of Meryton's less discerning figures.

Had Mr Darcy been privy to the clandestine plans concocted in his honour, Elizabeth was certain he would be incensed and affronted. In truth, she hoped there would be no need for their intervention. If her aspirations fell short, she could offer her apologies later and assert that she believed he, like her father, held scant regard for societal affairs. Consequently, she had endeavoured to shield him from its malevolent undercurrents. He already held her in low esteem, deeming her most improper —of which she was still sure in spite of her conflicted thoughts about the gentleman—and therefore, any further impropriety laid at her door could scarcely do her real harm.

*∧*∧*

Colonel Richard Fitzwilliam had scarcely arrived in the cosy Hertfordshire village of Meryton when he was urged by his cousin to attend the Assembly. Darcy made it clear that the good Colonel ought to attend post-haste to witness the young ladies, whose likeness to their aunt's kin was causing great consternation.

As a veteran of many a village soiree in the early years of his career, he knew precisely what to expect: rustic comportment, overzealous conviviality, and a slew of Mamas seized with the vapours and a fierce desire to wed off their unattached daughters.

The war had deprived most rural areas of eligible young men who were ever-eager to improve their fortunes on the battlefield. This, in turn, left the young ladies with precious few options, often driving them and their mothers to the brink of desperation and, at times, even subterfuge and blackmail to ensnare a husband. The arrival of not one but two eligible bachelors of means would no doubt set the town aflutter.

In a society such as this, the Colonel's noble family alone rendered him a desirable match in spite of his lack of pecuniary assets. As the second son of an earl, he was an excellent catch, particularly for a young lady with wealth but no rank. Undoubtedly, Meryton's society would have a handful of such ladies.

With any luck, there might even be agreeable young ladies with whom he could dance and converse with some degree of intelligence. Surely, they could not be any worse than the one cross-eyed shrew who had attempted to ensnare him in Scotland.

Armed with this thought, the Colonel felt adequately prepared for whatever the assembly might hold.

* ∧ * ∧ *

After dutifully partaking in a dance with Miss Bingley and offering a polite turn to Mrs Hurst, Darcy took his leave from the lively dance floor and sought solace in a secluded corner of the ballroom, from where he could discreetly observe the gathering. Naturally, Bingley had already engaged in two sets with the enchanting Miss Bennet, leaving Hurst to retire to the refreshment tables while Caroline and Louisa were enduring the insipid and naïve pleasantries of Sir William, the seemingly prominent figure in the local community.

Lady Lucas, it appeared, was fully engrossed in tending to her young sons while her daughters—the elder being plain, sensible, and undoubtedly past her prime, and the younger displaying nervous excitement yet possessing a certain delicate charm—mingled and danced in the company of other gentlemen.

A hint of amusement played upon Darcy's lips as he observed the bewildered countenance of Richard Fitzwilliam whilst he twirled about the dance floor with Miss Mary. Evidently, the Colonel had recognised the resemblance. The expression of astonishment had yet to fade from his countenance.

"Mr Darcy, might I offer you refreshments?" came the soft inquiry of Miss Elizabeth, jolting him from his keen observations. "Regrettably, there is no library present to entice you, but an excellent punch awaits, perfectly suited to cool one's throat after a lively dance."

Darcy glanced about, only to find that Miss Bingley had disengaged herself from the clutches of Sir William and was now making her way towards him. Providentially, a new set was assembling.

"Your kind offer, madam, is most appreciated. However, I must confess a much stronger inclination to inquire whether you would do me the honour of joining me in this forthcoming set."

With a smile and curtsey, she accepted his extended hand, a glimmer of mischief evident in her eyes. "You are truly kind, sir, to fulfil your obligation in light of the limited number of gentlemen available."

Leading her onto the dance floor and taking his position within one of the smaller sets, he declared, "I consider this a genuine pleasure."

As he bowed and she curtseyed to commence the dance, Miss Elizabeth murmured, "Even though I consort with sheep, sir?"

In spite of his best efforts to maintain composure, a smile crept across Darcy's countenance. "Especially so, madam," he replied in a dry tone. "One inevitably grows weary of the conventional amusements of the Ton after a certain period."

Arching an eyebrow at him, accompanied by a faint smile, she quipped, "Goodness, are all the gentlemen of the Ton so open-minded?"

A brief separation during the dance provided Darcy with a moment to compose a suitable response to her teasing— a teasing that he found peculiarly gratifying and intellectually stimulating. "Alas, no. Many confine themselves to more conventional pursuits, remaining oblivious to the pleasures that can be derived from animal husbandry."

While she maintained an outwardly composed demeanour, save for that mischievous smile, the laughter in her eyes spoke volumes about the lady's delight in his reply. "In that case, you must acknowledge that we rustic country folk have our unique sources of entertainment," she remarked with an underlying amusement.

Darcy's own smile broadened. "Indeed, madam, in that regard, I must concede. Although well-versed in the delights of Ovid and Plato, I had not anticipated finding such amusement among ovines."

"Amusements of the bovine variety are more prevalent in these parts, I confess, sir," Elizabeth smiled, her eyes twinkling mischievously. "Those, alas, are experiences you seem to know all too well."

Caught off guard by her astuteness and wit, Darcy marvelled at her presence in a place so removed from intellectual stimulation. How could she deliver such cutting judgments upon society at large and her own with such finesse, all without arousing suspicion?

"Indeed, your perception is strikingly accurate," he managed to say, concealing his burgeoning grin with great effort. "Clearly, your accomplishments would be the envy of an angel."

She blushed prettily, a delicate flush colouring her cheeks. "There is but one angel amongst my sisters, sir, and it appears your friend has claimed her for the evening."

Darcy could not help but agree with her assessment of Bingley's attachment to Miss Jane Bennet. "He ought to be persuaded to share, for it would be an unconscionably rude act to monopolise such a valuable creature."

A twitch of amusement graced Elizabeth's lips. "Your consideration for the well-being of others is truly commendable, sir."

"You bestow upon me more credit than I deserve," replied he. "I must confess to a certain selfishness, preferring to preserve my own comfort and shield myself from the wrath of aggrieved suitors seeking retribution for Mr Bingley's transgressions."

Their dance momentarily carried them apart, affording Darcy a brief respite to compose a suitable response to her teasing, which he found both delightful and intellectually invigorating.

"It is a truth universally acknowledged," said he eventually, "that the rustic country folk have their unique amusements, much to the bewilderment of the London society."

Her countenance remained composed, but the mirth in her eyes was unmistakable. "Indeed, sir, one can find amusement even in the simplest of pursuits. I dare say it is a virtue of the countryside."

Darcy felt a warmth spreading within him, ignited by the lively banter they shared. What an extraordinary woman she was, traversing the boundaries of societal expectations with her wit and intelligence. Truly, she was a breath of fresh air amidst the stifling conformity of the ton.

*∧*∧*

Having twirled around the ballroom with each of the four eligible Miss Bennets, Colonel Fitzwilliam was compelled to admit that Darcy's discernment had not been bewildered into perceiving resemblances to the de Bourgh family. Indeed, as his cousin had aptly noted, the resemblance was most remarkable in the case of Miss Mary, whose countenance bore an uncanny resemblance to Anne de Bourgh.

Had it been a mere coincidence, Fitzwilliam might have easily dismissed it as such. However, this was not the case. For in Miss Elizabeth, he found a striking similarity to the portrait of his own grandmother, the mother of Aunt Catherine.

A perplexing question nagged his mind. Why should the daughters of a modest country gentleman bear such an astonishing resemblance to a family with whom they seemingly had no connection? As Mrs Jannie Bennet had long since departed this world, Fitzwilliam had no means to coax from her any ancestral secrets that might lay hidden. The only certainty he could proffer was that her sister, Mrs Phillips, bore no semblance whatsoever to any of the Bennet girls, and the two Miss Phillipses displayed a lamentable lack of refinement. From either of them, the Colonel had garnered nought save an exhaustive list enumerating the imagined flaws of Miss Bennets.

In truth, dancing with these ill-mannered country damsels proved to be a respite from the intolerably condescending demeanour of Bingley's sisters. While the conduct of Mrs Hurst and Miss Bingley adhered strictly to propriety, they contrived to wound the sensibilities of all who dared approach them.

Fitzwilliam found it quite amusing to observe Darcy's artful avoidance whenever Miss Bingley found herself without a partner. The woman, it appeared, had failed to grasp the realisation that pursuing Darcy only served to push him further away, strengthening his resolve to evade any snares that may be set for him.

In contrast, the Bennet sisters seemed to comprehend Darcy's intentions perfectly and were actively aiding him in his pursuit, all the while exuding sweetness and innocence. Not only that, they also shielded him from the clutches of the most predatory Mamas and their ambitious daughters. Such seamless coordination of effort amongst them brought a great deal of delight to the Colonel, akin to witnessing a commander leading his troops with utmost efficiency and harmony.

*∧*∧*

Mr Darcy, with an air of composed elegance, escorted Miss Catherine away from the lively dance floor, only to be accosted by the ever-impertinent Miss Bingley, who addressed him with her customary audacity, saying, "You display such remarkable patience in enduring the relentless pursuit of these brazen young ladies, Mr Darcy."

The man's countenance stiffened, but before any unseemly utterances could escape his lips, Miss Catherine intervened, skilfully diffusing the mounting tension with an innocent inquiry. "Pray tell, Miss Bingley, do you truly envy a young lady's opportunity to shine on this auspicious occasion, which marks the pinnacle of her first season?"

The horror momentarily flickered across Caroline Bingley's countenance, and it took her a moment to regain her composure and reply with a forced smile, "Oh, no, Miss Catherine. I assure you, I harbour no such ill feelings. Mr Darcy is, indeed, gracious in bestowing his attention upon you during this momentous affair."

"Indeed, Miss Bingley, Mr Darcy's kindness extends even more notice to Mr Bingley's acquaintances than they perhaps deserve."

Caroline's countenance darkened at the subtle insult, for Kitty's innocent words seemed to imply a reference to herself rather than to Miss Bingley. The Colonel, who had overheard the exchange, could not help but admire the young lady for her cleverness and audacity.

Before he could intervene and endeavour to charm Caroline, Miss Elizabeth approached and addressed her thus, "Miss Bingley, I have heard of your exceptional talent on the pianoforte. Would you deign to demonstrate your skill while the musicians take respite?"

"I would be honoured, Miss Eliza," the woman responded, her smile betraying a triumphant air. "Mr Darcy, would you be so kind as to turn the pages for me?"

Though Darcy concealed his emotions with practised artistry surpassing that of most gentlemen, Fitzwilliam, being intimately acquainted with his cousin's temperament, could discern his reluctance to undertake this task. Yet, the dictates of courtesy compelled Darcy to acquiesce.

Drawing nearer to the two Bennet sisters, the Colonel overheard Miss Catherine's murmured query, "Does Miss Bingley truly require assistance with the pages?"

In equally hushed tones, her sister responded, "I do not believe Miss Bingley requires any aid, Kitty."

The Colonel stifled a chuckle, disguising it as a discreet clearing of his throat. "Miss Elizabeth, Miss Catherine, would you graciously consent to accompany a parched and weary soldier to partake of refreshments at the table?"

Both young ladies regarded him with a searching gaze,

attempting to ascertain whether they had been overheard making their less than complimentary remarks about Miss Bingley.

"We could hardly deny the company of one of England's gallant defenders," Miss Elizabeth remarked, a hint of mirth twinkling in her eyes.

Her sister quickly concurred, adding, "Indeed, the poor Colonel must be in dire need of refreshment."

"Oh, undoubtedly," he cheerfully agreed. "This ceaseless dancing is truly exhausting. I marvel at how delicate creatures like yourselves endure it."

Miss Elizabeth bestowed upon him a radiant smile. "For that, we are indebted to the excellent counsel of our dear mother, who advises us to walk no less than two miles each day, except in cases of illness when one should strive to walk as much as possible until longer walks can be resumed. It fortifies both our breath and limbs, you see." Her words carried a touch of playful imitation, clearly mimicking Mrs Bennet's prim demeanour.

Meanwhile, Miss Bingley commenced her performance, beginning with Mozart's Rondo Alla Turka. Though played with dazzling technical precision, the tempo was undeniably rushed. However, neither Miss Bennet uttered a word while she graced the keys, ensuring their complete attentiveness. Such small acts of courtesy towards a musician greatly intrigued the Colonel; amidst the bustling assembly hall, Miss Bingley could scarcely expect more than a cursory acknowledgement from those who deigned to listen.

As the final notes resonated, met with polite applause, Caroline embarked upon a sonata that Fitzwilliam privately believed she had chosen to showcase her own skill rather than to please her audience. His assessment was confirmed by the exchanged glance between the two Miss Bennets and the whispered comment of Miss Catherine, "I might find her playing more agreeable if it possessed a modicum of heartfelt sentiment.

It appears to be purely technical."

Miss Elizabeth responded in a similarly subdued tone, "Miss Bingley is undeniably proficient. It is a pity that she does not seem to derive any genuine pleasure from the music she performs."

"Indeed," Fitzwilliam interjected, his voice carefully modulated. "Technique without passion is preferable to passion without technique. A blending of both qualities would be most desirable."

The words hung in the air, a subtle acknowledgement of their shared understanding and discernment. The exchange concluded with a polite smile from Miss Elizabeth, an attempt to suppress her amusement entirely, yet her sparkling eyes betrayed a hint of mischief.

And so, the conversation continued in the language of subtle wit and genteel observations, the dance of words mirroring the graceful movements on the ballroom floor.

The Colonel found himself captivated by the intelligence and vivacity of the Bennet sisters, their playful banter and astute observations far surpassing the superficiality often encountered in such social gatherings. In this refined atmosphere, amidst the strains of music and the sophisticated exchanges, Fitzwilliam discovered a kindred spirit in Miss Elizabeth, her intellect and quick wit proving a delightful match to his own.

As soon as Miss Bingley concluded her chatter, Sir William loudly summoned Mary to play for a set of dances. Elizabeth hastened to join her sister at the pianoforte, for she had observed Mary appearing pale and worn. Her sister had never been fond of boisterous, cramped gatherings, however she did enjoy them to the extent that her health allowed before betraying her.

Mary's relieved smile upon her sister's arrival confirmed Lizzy's suspicion had been accurate.

Mary commenced with an original rustic composition, a

beloved melody in the area, and Elizabeth picked up the refrain. They soon lost themselves in the music, embellishing the dance as they often did when playing at home for their sisters' entertainment. Upon the end of the first dance, Lizzy played a soft bridging section while the dancers selected new partners before moving on to a chaconne.

They played many dances in this manner until the musicians returned from quenching their thirst and resting their fingers.

Elizabeth had no need to inquire if Mary required some fresh air. She knew her sister too well to question her need. Therefore, once they were freed of their musical duties, Lizzy aided her sister to the doors of the assembly hall and out into the moonlit night. Below, coachmen engaged in their own amusements, but all was hushed on the landing above the stairs.

Mary drew a few deep breaths. "Thank you, Lizzy. I would loathe to depart early because of my foolish ailments."

Elizabeth could not resist a smile. "I doubt Papa would regard it as an inconvenience."

"Oh, Papa would be delighted." Mary sighed. "I would not deprive Jane of Mr Bingley's company when she finds it so delightful, nor would I ruin Kitty's first assembly."

Elizabeth embraced her sister. "You must not overlook your own well-being, Mary."

Coming out in a hamlet as small as Meryton was more about transitioning from simple, girlish dresses and braids to mature hairstyles and fashion than a grand event. The Lucases were the sole family to hold balls for a daughter's debut, and those were scarcely more than assemblies held at Lucas Lodge. For Kitty, her first season was a series of firsts - her first fashionable gown, her first appearance at church as a young lady, her first attendance at one of Aunt Phillips's card parties, and now her first assembly. Lizzy mused it must be frightfully daunting to be presented at a grand ball and then attend any number of events from which one had previously been excluded.

Meryton's diminutive society made it far simpler for a young lady to debut. Children often accompanied their parents under their watchful eyes, observing if not actively participating in the adults' activities. While it would be unjust to curtail Kitty's first assembly, it would not be as significant a loss as depriving her of a debutante ball.

Not that Elizabeth did not comprehend Mary's reluctance to let her health deprive her sisters of enjoyment. She understood all too well, having often witnessed Mary's vexation with her own infirmity.

Though Mary had made considerable progress from the delicate child whose health must be continuously guarded, she was more easily fatigued than her sisters and found events like the assembly difficult to endure.

Mary smiled. "It is only the presence of so many individuals in such close quarters, Lizzy. A breath of fresh air provides some relief." Mary appeared almost ethereal in the luminous moonlight, less tethered to earthly concerns. "I fear I shall never find contentment in society."

"Then you must seek a place where your happiness lies," declared Lizzy. "You need not subject yourself to situations that strain your health."

"Ah, but how would I secure a husband to care for me when Papa is no longer here?" Mary shook her head. "Such is the way of life - we are presented with trials to overcome as well as virtues to cultivate."

"Misquoting Fordyce, Mary?" Elizabeth chuckled softly. "How exceedingly improper of you."

Mary joined in the laughter. "There is nought improper in taking the cloth and adapting it to oneself." She embraced her sister. "Oh, Lizzy, I shall sorely miss you once we are wed."

# Chapter 4

Colonel Fitzwilliam arose with the sun as he intended to engage in a private tête-à-tête with his cousin. In the Netherfield library, a room adorned with lesser splendour than that of Pemberley, but before he could further reflect on it, the Colonel discovered that Darcy had already awaited him.

Without hesitation, Darcy addressed his cousin, "Well?"

Fitzwilliam shook his head and responded, "You have conjured no figment of your imagination. As you previously surmised, the resemblance between Miss Mary Bennet and Anne is nothing short of remarkable." A mischievous grin played upon his countenance. "And I dare say, Miss Elizabeth bears a striking resemblance to our esteemed grandmother, Lady Mary."

Darcy blinked, the tension visibly dissipating from his frame. "I was beginning to fear the frailty of my mind," uttered he, speaking into the air. Then, addressing Fitzwilliam, he continued, "Lady Mary? Pray, her memory eludes me."

Amusement danced in the Colonel's eyes as he chuckled, saying, "It is hardly surprising. It is unlikely that you had been apprised of the fact that our grandmother had had quite a reputation."

"Reputation?"

Wagging a finger playfully, Fitzwilliam admonished his cousin, "Your infrequent visits to our home hindered you from discovering our family's secret.

"I beg your pardon?"

"She was a wonderful woman, according to my father; however, you would hear many rumours within Ashfield's walls which suggested our dear grandmother had enjoyed the company of men more than a lady of her station perhaps should."

"What are you implying, Richard?"

"Nothing, for those, are only rumours, and one cannot confirm them one way or another. My father, in particular, would admonish you from even mentioning them."

"But what does this have to do with Miss Bennets' similarity to de Bourgh?"

"Nothing because it may have more to do with Fitzwilliams," the Colonel confessed, his grin widening unreservedly. "There exists a portrait of Lady Mary, painted soon after her nuptials. Your Miss Elizabeth could very well be her sister."

"She is scarcely mine," Darcy protested, his voice filled with indignation.

Fitzwilliam nearly succumbed to laughter, endeavouring to restrain himself lest he awoke the entire household of Netherfield. "Come now, cousin. I beheld the way in which you regarded her. And you must concede that she orchestrated her sisters with the finesse of a seasoned general, ensuring you were spared the most insidious fortune-seeking mamas and their progeny."

Darcy spluttered, his speech impeded until he managed to articulate his thoughts. "She..." He shook his head. "I cannot assert that I am ungrateful, but—"

"Pray, do not falter," the Colonel interjected, clasping his cousin's shoulder with enough force to disorientate the more delicate man. "I, too, was compelled to dance with some of those mercenary vixens. Be grateful that Miss Bingley's company was the worst you endured." Shaking his head, he pondered aloud, "Is there no familial connection to be found between the Bennets and our esteemed lineage?"

Darcy shook his head, a gesture filled with resignation. "None, I am afraid. I encountered their aunt, Mrs Phillips and her daughters. The late Mrs Bennet also had a brother named Gardiner, a tradesman residing in London. I think I mentioned him in my letter."

"Indeed." Fitzwilliam furrowed his brow, deep in thought. "That Gardiner name rings a bell, though I cannot ascertain its origin." He shook his head, dismissing the elusive memory. "I shall dispatch an express to my father detailing what we know thus far. Perhaps he and Mother shall contain further insight."

The Colonel harboured no doubt that a connection existed. Unravelling such an association would provide a diverting diversion from the mundane matters of liaising with the young and inexperienced Captain Denny of the militia.

With a polite inclination of his head, Darcy acknowledged his cousin's determination. "Your initiative is commendable, Fitzwilliam. I trust your endeavour shall produce sufficient results." A hint of gratitude laced his words.

Now satisfied with his purpose, the Colonel straightened his posture and clasped his hands behind his back. "I will make haste in composing the missive. We shall not tarry in our pursuit of answers." A gleam of excitement sparkled in his eyes.

Upon Fitzwilliam's corroboration of his suspicions, Darcy found that partaking in breakfast with his friend's family was nothing short of a taxing ordeal. Bingley himself exuded an air of amiable charm, while Hurst, on the other hand, contributed nought but mere appreciation for the victuals before them. However, in their infinite wisdom, Mrs Hurst and Miss Bingley elected to flavour their discourse with scornful commentary on the society and inhabitants of Meryton.

This impropriety caused Bingley to redden with discomfort, though he chose to maintain his silence until Caroline embarked upon a thorough catalogue of the various faults possessed by the Bennet girls. With an air of mirthful amusement, she accused them of deceitful conduct, feigning affluence through donning fashionable gowns while it was common knowledge that their means were meagre. She further disparaged their lowly connections and their apparent lack of decorum, deeming such insignificant creatures unworthy of any societal standing.

Casting a brief glance at his cousin, Darcy pondered whether he, too, yearned for Bingley to assert his authority over his sister. Indeed, the Colonel's sombre countenance appeared to mirror Darcy's sentiments.

Only when Miss Bingley set her sights upon Miss Jane Bennet did Bingley interject with a plea, "Caroline, that shall suffice. If you cannot utter words of civility, you should refrain from speaking altogether."

For a protracted moment, Miss Bingley stared at her brother, her mouth agape in a most unseemly manner. With a decisive snap of her jaws, she redirected her attention to the consumption of her morning repast.

The ensuing sulky silence proved far more agreeable than a breakfast peppered with malevolence.

Darcy experienced a palpable sense of relief when Bingley broached the subject of his interview with the tenants, proposing that he and the Colonel accompany him.

*∧*∧*

At Longbourn, an air of contentment prevailed. Mr Bennet's customary acerbic humour concerning the society of Meryton lay dormant, for he was as delighted as his daughters by the prospect that Jane had seemingly captured the attention of a gentleman whom she herself esteemed, which was leading to a potential genuine affection.

Now, observing his daughters revelling in Jane's triumph while lamenting their inability to fully safeguard Mr Darcy from the clutches of the more predatory ladies at the gathering, Mr Bennet pondered if those arduous years of perpetual disappointment had not eroded his own spirit. Once upon a time, he had danced with the same fervour as any gentleman and taken great pride in accompanying Mrs Bennet, as well as Jannie, onto the ballroom floor.

Perhaps he should have shown greater sympathy and refrained from allowing his own indolence and perplexity to drive him towards the refuge of his library.

Perhaps.

But such regrets were futile, as he could not alter the past.

It was better to partake in his daughters' joys and make the most of the time when he would remain the sole male presence in their lives. Jane's partiality towards Mr Bingley made it evident that time was limited. Soon enough, the others would find suitable husbands and depart to start their new families.

"Are you in good spirits, Papa?" inquired Lizzy. "You do not seem quite yourself."

He dismissed his amusement at his foolishness and offered his favourite daughter a smile. "No, Lizzy, all is well." He must discipline his own mind. How absurd to grow maudlin over a young gentleman's partiality for Jane's company.

Mrs Bennet sized the opportunity to chimp in, "I must say, Miss Bingley's performance was awe-inspiring."

"She played with great skill, I am sure," acknowledged Jane.

"Oh, indeed, exceedingly well." Elizabeth smiled mischievously, her eyes glimmering with mischief. "It is a pity, though, that she seemed not to derive any enjoyment from her own performance."

Mary arched an eyebrow. "I dare say, the quality of Miss Bingley's taste speaks for itself."

Lydia stifled her laughter. "Oh, that orange!" she uttered under her breath.

Catching wind of her youngest daughter's remark, Mrs Bennet declared, "There is nothing inherently amiss with the colour. However, I must concede that it was not a flattering choice for the lady in question. That particular hue is best employed as an accent, as only a select few possess the complexion to wear it to advantage." She nodded to her girls. "Your wisdom is sound, even if one ought not to voice criticism, even in private."

Elizabeth raised an eyebrow. "How, then, are we to attain a deeper understanding, Mama? Does not comprehending emerge from thoughtful critique?"

Even Jane struggled to conceal her laughter. Lizzy seldom teased their mother, but it proved an enthralling spectacle when she did.

Mrs Bennet, quite unexpectedly, graced her second daughter with a smile. "The line is indeed fine, Lizzy, as you know from the numerous occasions you have deftly tread upon it without crossing over."

Mr Bennet made a deliberate effort to appear disinterested, as he had astonishingly found himself startled. He had been married to Camila for over fifteen years, never fully acknowledging the woman's razor-sharp wit.

Elizabeth theatrically dabbed her lips with her napkin. "You are most gracious, Mama. However, what of those who are still acquiring the ways of society? How shall they gain enlightenment?"

Once again, that almost smile graced Mrs Bennet's slender countenance. "The conventional method applies, Lizzy. One learns by venturing, faltering, and bearing the consequences."

Mr Bennet observed the lively exchange with a sense of contentment. In spite of the weight of past disappointments, he found solace in the spirited banter of Camila with the girls. The challenges of society and the fleeting nature of happiness were ever-present. Still, in these moments, surrounded by their vibrant personalities, he knew that a certain kind of joy could be found amidst the trials of life.

Perhaps he should go out more often from his library.

*∧*∧*

As the Bennet family sat down to break their fast the next morning, Mr Bennet was suddenly summoned by the arrival of a post express. Upon his return, he held an opened letter with a countenance that conveyed both puzzlement and amusement.

"My dears," said he in a tone that was nothing short of astonishment, "It appears that we shall have a visitor this very evening. By some inexplicable means," he continued, "Mr Collins has decided to mend the breach between our families." He paused for a moment and added, "It would seem that my cousin's son has a more favourable view of the entail than his father."

Elizabeth was left to ponder what sort of absurdity this unknown cousin had concocted while Mr Bennet re-examined the letter. "Perhaps it is best if I simply read the letter and allow you to form your own opinions," he suggested.

Lizzy remained silent. She knew that her father would read the letter regardless of their protests. Although Kitty and Lydia were eager for him to do so, and Mary had dutifully expressed her interest, Elizabeth was well aware that their father's delight came from amusing himself at the expense of others. In spite of wishing that he would refrain from such a pastime, she knew better than to expect him to change his ways.

According to the letter, Mr Collins had recently been distinguished by the patronage of Lady Catherine de Bourgh, whose bounty and beneficence has preferred him to the valuable rectory of this parish in Hunsford.

Elizabeth wondered if Lady Catherine was the mother of Mr Darcy's cousin, Anne, whose resemblance to Mary had caused the gentleman such offence. Indeed, could there be two de Bourgh families with daughters named Anne? It was coincidence enough that their cousin Collins should be affiliated with one.

However, the question that perplexed Elizabeth was why Mr Collins divulged many personal details in his letter to people he had never seen. She searched in vain for a satisfactory answer. The only explanation she could conceive was that his adoration for his noble patroness had reached an almost blasphemous level of idolatry. This unfavourable impression of Mr Collins cast doubt upon his professed motives for acquainting himself with his cousins, suggesting that he was, at best feeble-minded and, at worst, a sycophantic individual.

Mr Collins sought a wife and perceived the plentiful daughters of Longbourn as both a favourable matrimonial prospect and a means to reunite the two branches of their family.

Lizzy could not fault his intention, for if one of her sisters were to capture his heart, they would all be spared the apprehension of losing their home should their father pass away before their marriages were secured.

In spite of the preposterous nature of his letter, Elizabeth held out hope that the man might prove agreeable in person. Perhaps he was simply one of those men who struggled to express themselves adequately in writing. Surely, penning a missive requesting to mend the divide between the two branches of the family was no easy task. She resolved not to allow her initial impression to taint her judgment of the man and decided to withhold final judgment until she had gained more knowledge.

"Well, my dears?" Mr Bennet inquired upon concluding the reading, seeking his family's opinions.

"While it would surely disappoint you, Papa, I hope Mr Collins possesses more sense than his epistle suggests," responded Elizabeth. "Though his noble goal of reuniting our family deserves admiration, it would be challenging for any of us to rally behind a man of truly ridiculous nature."

"Indeed, a man of the cloth ought to embody worthiness," Mary nodded solemnly; a hint of amusement escaped her voice and sparkled in her eyes. "In spite of his unfortunate talent for letter writing."

Lydia laughed. "In that case, he is all yours, for I am exceedingly grateful that I am not eligible!"

Mrs Bennet frowned. "To form a strong aversion based solely on a single letter is unwise, Lydia. The gentleman may simply be an inept correspondent."

Lizzy had never heard her mother express such strong disapproval. Clearly, the ridiculous letter had unsettled her as well.

"I wonder if his patron's family is the same as Mr Darcy's cousin," she pondered. "De Bourgh is such an uncommon name that it seems highly unlikely for there to be more than one family bearing it."

"Perhaps you would like to consult Burke's Peerage, Lizzy?" suggested Mr Bennet. "Lady Catherine de Bourgh must assuredly be distinguished."

Rather than responding to the mischievousness in her father's tone, Lizzy replied with feigned modesty, "That would be prudent, Papa. We would not want any unpleasant surprises, after all."

*∧*∧*

Mr Collins lived up to the extraordinary nature of his missive, embodying a peculiar combination of servility and inflated self-importance. He offered insincere praise while comparing everything to the manners of his noble patroness, thereby negating any attempt at flattery.

If that were not enough, the clergyman exhibited such

a lack of attention to his appearance that his countenance bore blemishes, his hair was lank and oily, and his clothing was dishevelled. When Elizabeth found herself thinking he resembled a black stork caught in a tempest, she must stifle her laughter and disguise it as a coughing fit while attempting to divert Mr Collins from his unwelcome eulogy on the delicate health of ladies.

Before Elizabeth could intervene, Mary deftly diverted the conversation, rescuing her from the uncomfortable exchange. "Do you indulge in the works of Fordyce, Mr Collins?"

Leaning in towards Mary, the man smiled. "Indeed, Miss Mary—or may I say, Cousin Mary? I find Fordyce to be an invaluable reference on the nature of humanity and the lamentable ease with which one may deviate from the path of virtue." He puffed himself up, resembling the very stork Elizabeth had envisioned earlier. "In fact, I have often incorporated references to Fordyce's works in my own sermons, much to the delight of Lady."

Suppressing their laughter, the sisters engaged in a silent battle to keep their mirth at bay, except for Mary, who maintained an ability of a perfectly composed countenance while listening to such a statement.

Her eyes sparkled with amusement, though her voice and expression remained gravely composed as she replied, "Do you not believe, sir, that Fordyce places excessive emphasis on societal strictures rather than focusing on scriptural teachings? As someone who has received a formal education in divinity—certainly far greater than any I can claim—it appears to me that when addressing matters of morality, one's primary reference should be the Bible."

Elizabeth revised her earlier comparison of Mr Collins to a stork, realising he resembled a bedraggled blackfish, mouth agape as it gasped for air.

"You astonish me, Cousin Mary!" he sounded genuinely

astounded. "I had not expected to encounter such scholarly discourse in such pleasant company."

"Oh, Papa is indeed quite the scholar," Mary replied with a smile. "We have all spent a great deal of time in his library. Perhaps you would appreciate perusing the books that align with your interests?"

The gentleman glanced around the parlour. "If my esteemed cousins do not object, I would be honoured to retire to the library. However—" He hesitated, perhaps struck by a newfound sense of self-awareness.

Mary laughed. "Oh, Longbourn's library could never rival Rosings, Mr Collins. However, it is far more accessible to you now, and considering Papa's own scholarly inclinations, it may contain books better suited to your tastes. After all, the de Bourghs must have filled their library according to their own preferences."

Lizzy managed to restrain herself until the parlour door closed, and then she allowed her laughter to escape in subdued bursts.

When she finally regained composure and glanced apologetically at her sisters, she discovered that they all, even Jane, had tears of mirth streaming down their faces.

Shaking her head, Elizabeth admitted, "I know it is unkind to laugh so heartily, for the man has clearly faced great disappointment in his life. But oh, what an extraordinary creature he is!"

Kitty looked around mischievously before launching into an amusing imitation of their cousin's demeanour. "Why, Cousin Elizabeth, I declare Lady Catherine de Bourgh would never allow anyone under her care to experience disappointment."

"Kitty, please!" Jane pleaded, her voice strained as if on the verge of choking.

After escorting her cousin to her father's library, Mary returned to the parlour, her face flushed and tears still glistening in her eyes. "Oh, I must never engage in such cruelty again," confessed she, dropping gracelessly onto the settee. "Life has been undeniably unkind to our cousin. He was so grateful for the freedom of Papa's library that he forgot to mention Rosings Park."

Taking a slow, steadying breath, Elizabeth replied, "Then he has indeed suffered, Mary? The man who incessantly heaps praise upon others appears... well..."

Mary nodded, her demeanour growing serious. "Mr Collins's father could neither read nor write. I gather he was not a benevolent man. His son learned in secret, receiving lessons from his mother, who concealed it from her husband. Later, he attended the village school when his father deceased. He earned a scholarship to enter the seminary."

With that concise account, Elizabeth's imagination filled in the gaps. It was no wonder Mr Collins displayed such a curious blend of inflated pride and obsequious flattery. The poor man must have spent much of his life in a state of perpetual fear. She chastised herself for finding amusement at his expense.

"We must endeavour to show kindness," Jane interjected, her voice wavering slightly. "Perhaps his manners will... improve as he gains confidence."

Elizabeth nodded, though she could not help but think that poor Mr Collins was unlikely to become any more bearable.

The next morning, the Bennet ladies sauntered into the pleasant town of Meryton in the company of their cousin. With an ardent desire to ascertain the arrival of the books she had recently procured, Elizabeth sought solace in the prospect of reading her new literary acquisitions. Jane, on the other hand, wanted fresh ribbons to adorn her finest bonnet, and Mary, a fervent admirer of music, nurtured hopes of discovering new sheets in the esteemed bookshop of Meryton. As for Kitty and Lydia, their youthful curiosity and fondness for fashion compelled them to seize any opportunity that might present itself to explore the latest fabrics and bonnets on offer.

Given Mr Collins' expressed interest in their promenade and the literary emporium, it followed naturally that he should accompany them. Despite his evident unfamiliarity with exertion, not a complaint escaped his lips. Indeed, in Elizabeth's estimation, he seemed to possess an air of thoughtfulness. Frequently, his gaze strayed towards Mary, accompanied by a fleeting shadow of concern that appeared on his countenance before being swiftly banished.

Meryton was abuzz with excitement owing to the encampment of a militia regiment a mere two miles away. Young officers had already begun captivating the hearts of Meryton's matrons. While a wealthy gentleman might be deemed a suitable match, the advent of a dashing officer in red uniforms endowed with promising prospects invariably ignited a far more thrilling prospect in young ladies' hearts.

"Pray, look!" Kitty exclaimed, gesturing towards a cluster of officers. "Is that not Frank Denny? How he has matured!"

Indeed, young Denny appeared far more imposing than Elizabeth recollected. The uniform befitted him well, and his once boyish moustache had blossomed into a resplendent emblem of manly refinement. Not only had his frame filled out, but he had also grown taller.

Catherine sighed wistfully. "He appears exceedingly handsome," murmured she, "an image far removed from the mischievous boy who once tugged at my plaits during a church service."

Mary, Jane, and Mr Collins having no inclination towards officers in general or Denny in particular, directed their steps towards the bookshop, leaving Elizabeth behind to ensure that her mother would not be overwhelmed by the exuberance of

Kitty and Lydia. Lizzy could attend to her own purchases once the commotion had subsided.

Astutely aware of their presence, Denny extricated himself from the company of officers and approached with a deferential bow when he drew near enough for conversation. "Mrs Bennet, Miss Elizabeth, Miss Catherine, Miss Lydia, what a pleasure it is to behold old acquaintances from our beloved hometown looking so resplendent."

The women exchanged curtseys in unison.

"You, too, possess a countenance of remarkable vitality, Mr Denny," Kitty responded, her countenance graced by a winsome smile. "Army life seems to agree with you."

As decorum dictated, Lydia retired to her mother's side, yet her longing to partake in the conversation was palpable.

"Captain Denny," he corrected with a responsive smile, his visage emanating with well-earned pride. "I received my promotion orders a mere two days hence."

"Allow me to extend my congratulations, Captain," interjected Elizabeth, ensuring her tone conveyed nothing more than conventional civility. "It affords me immense pleasure to witness one of Meryton's sons advancing in his station."

Denny's grin, ever sincere and infectious, adorned his countenance. "Opportunities abound for a young man eager to make his mark, Miss Lizzy."

"Pray tell, Denny, are you monopolising all the fair maidens for yourself?" A smooth tenor voice interjected from behind. Presently, a handsome young gentleman, devoid of regimentals, emerged and bestowed an engaging smile upon the gathering.

Denny shook his head, a playful glimmer in his eye. "Excuse my friend, for he has recently acquired a commission but has yet to receive his uniform. Wickham, allow me to introduce Mrs Bennet and her three daughters, Miss Bennet, Miss Catherine, and Miss Lydia."

Elizabeth arched an eyebrow with a hint of scepticism. "I

was under the impression that the mere possession of a uniform did not confer immediate propriety." She maintained a light and playful tone, eager to probe Wickham's intentions, which appeared rather dubious.

"Nay, indeed it does not," Mr Wickham conceded with a graceful bow. "But can a man be faulted for being momentarily struck mute in the presence of such dazzling beauty?"

Elizabeth executed a demure curtsey. "Once he tenders his apologies, forgiveness may be bestowed," she conceded, unable to suppress a barely stifled giggle from Lydia's direction.

Wickham's smile broadened. "Then I must humbly apologise for my sins, for the opportunity to gain forgiveness from a captivating lady such as yourself must surely rival the most ardent desires."

A charming rogue, Elizabeth inwardly surmised. "Your apology is accepted, sir," she declared, veiling her true sentiments beneath a composed facade. Wickham, however, failed to inspire unreserved trust, though the precise cause of her reservations eluded her.

As she discerned the approaching cadence of hoofbeats, her delicate ears attuned to the sound, Denny interjected, "Methinks the Colonel's long-awaited aid is nigh." The young gentleman bestowed a genial smile. "Colonel Forster, having but recently ascended to his current station, is embarking upon his maiden mission. Colonel Fitzwilliam from the regulars shall serve as his sage adviser throughout the ensuing months."

Wickham, startled, blinked and involuntarily grew pallid. Casting a fleeting glance towards the oncoming equestrians, he discreetly swallowed. "I must now take my leave," he declared. "It has been an honour to make your acquaintance, ladies."

Elizabeth's lips pursed contemplatively as she beheld the man's retreating figure. Though he seemed to stroll leisurely, an uncharacteristic stealth marked his gait as he sought refuge within the shadows cast by towering edifices or mingled amidst clusters of individuals until he vanished from her sight. How exceedingly peculiar.

Denny extended his hands in resignation. "Regrettably, I, too, must make my departure." With a courteous bow, he added, "Colonel Forster shall undoubtedly require the presence of his subordinates."

Thus, they exchanged their farewells, and Mrs Bennet repaired to the haberdashery with her youngest girls, leaving Lizzy to seek solace within the sanctuary of the book emporium.

Elizabeth's heart yearned to converse with Jane, for there was an unsettling element about the brief encounter that troubled her deeply.

She was before the door of the bookstore when she heard a call.

"Miss Bennet?"

She stopped and turned gracefully towards the mellifluous timbre of Mr Darcy's voice, curtsying with poise. "Good day, Mr Darcy."

A flicker of a smile momentarily graced the gentleman's austere countenance. "I wanted to express my gratitude to you and your sisters for the attentiveness you displayed in ensuring my felicity at the assembly." He doffed his hat. "Given our shared objective, I deemed this an opportune moment to extend my appreciation."

"I am obliged, sir." Elizabeth's countenance softened with a smile. "Though I cannot vouch for Meryton as the epitome of all your desires, Mr Brooks does maintain an esteemed establishment. Should you choose to extend your sojourn, he shall gladly procure any literary or material acquisition you may choose."

Once again, Darcy's lips betrayed a suppressed inclination to smile, yet he valiantly resisted. "This intelligence proves invaluable, for I confess that Netherfield's library is rather lacking in substance."

He held the door open.

Lizzy accepted the gesture with a graceful nod and ventured into the bookshop. "I am certain that my father would gladly grant you unfettered access to his library, should you be so inclined to make the request. He has already afforded a similar privilege to our cousin, Mr Collins, who made an unexpected visit from Hunsford."

In the subdued illumination of the establishment, Darcy's countenance appeared to harden. "Hunsford? Does it not house the living at Rosings Park?"

"Indeed," Elizabeth assented. "Mr Collins holds Rosings in the highest esteem, as well as its esteemed mistress."

Her observation left no room for doubt: Mr Darcy was distinctly displeased.

Darcy beheld Elizabeth with rapt attention, her graceful strides carrying her effortlessly towards the counter where she made inquiry of the clerk concerning her order. The gentleman's stomach remained taut, and though he longed to clench his fists, he suppressed the urge.

To witness that scoundrel Wickham in conversation with her had been vexing enough. However, the lady's frown upon the rogue's departure somewhat reassured him that she had not been easily taken in by his charming façade and silver tongue.

Alas, the discovery that his aunt's rector had paid a visit and, worse yet, was related to the Bennet family was too much to bear. Lady Catherine's fervent desire to see him betrothed to her daughter Anne had gone too far.

Darcy had nothing but fondness for his cousin, but his affections for her were akin to those he held for his sister. Anne de Bourgh was his equal in every respect, but her frail health and the intemperance of her mother made it imperative that she receive the utmost care. Unlike his sister, whose robust health and passion for outdoor activities like horseback riding kept her strong and resilient, Anne was in need of greater attention and concern.

A sigh escaped Darcy's lips, and he could not help but feel that the world conspired against him.

Miss Elizabeth's dulcet tones interrupted Darcy's thoughts.

"He appeared quite amicable on the surface, Mary, but there is something in him that I mistrust. Something... false."

Mary Bennet pondered her sister's words before replying, "And did he not hasten away in a furtive manner when Mr Denny mentioned Colonel Fitzwilliam? It strikes me as odd for a man who has only just purchased his commission. Surely he would desire the chance to display his prowess before a superior officer?"

So, Wickham had joined the militia, mused Darcy. That explained his presence in this locale, though it was a cruel twist of fate. Fitzwilliam would ensure that Forster knew to keep a close eye on him.

Many men purchased commissions to absolve some stain on their reputation or that of their family. If Wickham intended to redeem himself, then perhaps this was the course he had chosen.

Darcy could not fathom anything so magnanimous. Typically, the militia assignment lasted up to three months, ample time for a man to amass an unpaid debt or worse before absconding without a trace.

He knew he must speak with Mr Bennet and apprise him of his daughters' vulnerability. Though Bennet possessed no great fortune, there were others in the vicinity who did. Darcy was confident that Bennet knew to whom his warning should be heeded.

That left but one thing - controlling his temper. Darcy wondered if the arduous labours of Heracles might be easier than this.

# Chapter 5

Elizabeth inhaled deeply as she traversed the countryside, relishing the crisp scent of rain-washed air. Having been confined indoors for two consecutive days due to the typical showers of early autumn, she found great delight in venturing out on Hertfordshire lands.

It was anticipated that Jane would return from her sojourn to Netherfield in the afternoon, having departed before the storm struck, safely escorted by Martin Hill, who had nearly completed half of the journey homeward.

Lizzy harboured hopes that her sister had derived pleasure from her visit, though she suspected that, placed in Jane's stead, she would have found the company of Mrs Hurst and Miss Bingley rather tedious at best. Indeed, it was a stroke of fortune that she herself had not been extended a similar invitation.

Something stirred on the road up ahead, prompting Elizabeth to rein in Blackberry, even though her pace was measured enough to evade most unforeseen surprises. The presence of young children among the tenants meant that their actions could be somewhat unpredictable.

Gradually, the figure materialised into view—a boy of perhaps ten years, sprinting with all the vigour his young legs could muster. There seemed to be no immediate threat pursuing him, though as he drew nearer, Lizzy discerned the unmistakable mark of panic etched upon his countenance.

"Miss Lizzy!" The boy skidded to a halt near Blackberry. "Miss, could ye come straightaway to Ma's? Something dreadful has befallen our Maggie."

Rather than dwelling upon the nature of the unfortunate event, Elizabeth merely nodded and urged Blackberry into a gallop. Young Jimmie Waters would not be so agitated unless the need were genuinely urgent.

Lily, Mrs Waters' eleven-year-old daughter, stood anxiously at the entrance of their modest cottage, her hands tightly clasped within her apron. "Ma's tending to Maggie in the back, Miss Lizzy," the girl relayed as Elizabeth.

She hastened through the well-ordered home until she reached the bedroom, where Mrs Waters knelt beside the bed, her head bowed, and her shoulders convulsed with sobs.

"Mrs Waters?"

The woman scrambled to her feet. "Miss Lizzy! Is there... is there anything you can do?" She gestured towards the bed before wiping her eyes with her apron. "My John discovered her this mornin' by the Millbridge road. She's..." Her voice trailed off, and she buried her face in her apron, trembling. "My Maggie's a virtuous girl, Miss Lizzy. She would never engage in such abominable conduct..."

Elizabeth drew nearer, her breath catching in her throat at the sight that beheld her. In times past, Maggie Waters, a fourteen years old girl, may have possessed a certain loveliness, but if she were to survive this ordeal, beauty would forever elude her grasp. Her countenance was marred by bruising and severe swelling, and bandages bore testimony to even more grievous injuries. Elizabeth had to suppress a surge of nausea before she could muster a quivering voice and inquire, "Are you implying that she has been violated?"

Mrs Waters nodded, still convulsed with tremors. "She is a pure-hearted girl."

"No blame shall be attached to her," said Elizabeth. "I am uncertain as to what can be done for Maggie, Mrs Waters, but rest assured that your family shall neither endure shame nor punishment. You bear burdens aplenty."

*∧*∧*

Leaning against the wall outside her father's study, Elizabeth longed for nothing more than to retreat to her bedchamber and succumb to the solace of tears. Yet, before she could in good conscience seek that respite, there remained one final duty that demanded fulfilment.

Having aided Mrs Waters in the arduous task of cleansing and tending to her daughter's wounds—such was the mother's anguish that it rendered her incapable of coherent thought—Lizzy had entrusted the care of the younger children to her instructions, should any need arise. She had then informed the women who had learned of Maggie Waters's dire plight that they were not to venture forth unaccompanied, dispatching them to spread the news amongst the other tenants. Finally, she had returned to Longbourn, summoning the doctor to attend to Maggie's injuries and enlisting Mrs Hill's assistance in providing sustenance for the Waters family in their time of need.

Cold anger fueled Elizabeth throughout these tasks, but now, as she stood on the precipice of sharing the grim tidings with her parents, her ire faltered, leaving behind only weariness of the soul.

Upon receiving news of the terrible fate that had befallen young Waters, Mrs Bennet hurried to find Elizabeth. She knew that the incident must have profoundly affected her innocent mind in spite of the girl's intelligence. Upon seeing her, Lizzy stumbled towards her mother, struggling to hold back tears and maintain composure. She poured out the sordid details of what happened to Maggie, barely able to contain her emotions. Mrs Bennet embraced her tightly, just as she used to when Lizzy was a little girl.

Once she calmed down a bit, Mrs Bennet led them to Mr Bennet's library.

The man reclined in his cherished armchair, a timeworn relic adorned with faded upholstery that he adamantly refused to have reupholstered.

"Lizzy?" He lifted his gaze, his countenance fraught with apprehension as he saw her tearful, being held close by Mrs Bennet. "Lizzy? My goodness, what has happened?"

He jumped to his feet, and he and his wife guided their daughter to a seat, and Mr Bennet placed a small glass in her hand. "Consume it, Lizzy. It shall provide solace."

Elizabeth detected the scent of her father's brandy, yet imbibed nonetheless, coughing slightly as the potent spirit seared her throat all the way down to her stomach. Indeed, it steadied her nerves, imbuing the whole ordeal with a sense of distance, though no less horrendous. "Thank you, Papa."

Mrs Bennet told him everything that had happened to the daughter of one of their tenants, relating everything she had heard from Hill and imploring him to procure firm measures to protect all the girls in the neighbourhood.

The man settled into a neighbouring chair. For once, his usual air of mild absentmindedness was replaced by sombre indignation.

"I must consult with the magistrate and talk to other families in the area," said he. "And you, Lizzy, you must not venture alone for now." He sighed wearily. "I shall confer with Hill regarding the assignment of a few sturdy lads to safeguard the Waters family. As word spreads, the wretch may deem it necessary to ensure his victim remains incapable of disclosing anything about him."

Mrs Bennet looked at her husband with a combination of curiosity and gratification. It had been a while since her husband had shown any interest in anything beyond his library. However, the situation was severe indeed, and Thomas Bennet was not a bad man. He was just indolent.

Lizzy's breath caught in her throat. Such vile considerations had not crossed her mind. Her father patted her hand. "I lament this unfortunate incident, which has exposed you, my dearest Lizzy, to the basest of men." He shook his head ruefully, nodding to his wife to escort Elizabeth to her bedchamber and talk with other girls about what had happened.

Under different circumstances, Elizabeth would have objected; however, as she found no strength to do anything but lay in her bed and cry, she allowed her mother to assist her to her room.

"Are you sure you shall be well, Lizzy?" Mrs Bennet asked after guiding her daughter to her bed.

"I shall, Mama," she assured her. "You must go and talk to my sisters before they hear it from anyone else. They are too fragile to hear such an atrocity from anyone but you."

*∧*∧*

Elizabeth awoke with a throbbing head and a bitter taste lingering in her mouth, remnants of her daytime slumber. Nightmares featuring a faceless malefactor had left her chilled to the bone, and she trembled involuntarily.

One remedy existed, regardless of its impropriety, which could shield her from the perils of such men. If – heaven forbid – the need should arise, she would confront the consequences when they presented themselves. It was preferable to endure infamy for dispatching a would-be assailant than to suffer violation due to her inability to defend herself.

With this resolve at the forefront of her mind, Lizzy donned her oldest gown and made her way to the stables, where she extracted her flintlock pistol from her saddlebags. The solid weight of the weapon in her hand offered reassurance.

Elizabeth possessed an intimate understanding of the

firearm, from priming to firing. Circumstances had proved her proficiency, for on more than one occasion, she had rescued an inexperienced cowherd from an unruly bull with aspirations beyond his station. If she could have brought down such a creature while mounted at full gallop, she could surely dispatch a monster disguised as a man.

The only distinction, she reasoned, was that the cowherd's kin did not receive the gift of twenty pounds of prime beef afterwards.

Though her stomach refused to accept this rationale, Elizabeth felt safer with the flintlock in her possession. The task of cleaning, loading, and priming it daily, rather than weekly, might prove tiresome, but the price was well worth the assurance it provided.

Now, her mind was consumed with devising a means to keep the weapon with her at all times.

Lost in contemplation, Lizzy retraced her steps back to her chamber. The flintlock proved too weighty for a reticule and too conspicuous to be concealed within the folds of her attire.

Elizabeth embarked on a fervent search within the confines of her bedroom, her countenance brightening with a wistful smile upon the discovery of the timeworn receptacle she once had employed to collect polished pebbles from the babbling brook adjoining the hunting fields. Its sturdy frame possessed an enduring charm, which could be transformed into a modest yet rustic reticule of unmistakable allure with a delicate touch of muslin. The perfection of the find delighted her discerning eye.

Tenderly nestling the flintlock within its cosy confines, she descended the staircase, the basket held firmly in her grasp, as she prepared to join her sisters in the family gathering.

Though her entrance prompted a fleeting moment of surprise among her sisters, not a word concerning the basket or its enigmatic contents escaped their lips. Conversation faltered and stumbled as if tiptoeing around a well-guarded secret while

Lizzy deftly laboured to conceal the true purpose of her chosen vessel.

All the Bennet girls, in their own way, endeavoured to divert their thoughts from the unfortunate victim. Even the typically verbose Mr Collins, blessedly subdued by the recent tragedy, wisely refrained from mentioning either the basket or Lizzy's discreet activities. Instead, after an uncomfortably prolonged silence, he summoned the courage to address Mary, treading a precarious line between audacity and decorum.

"Permit me, dear Cousin Mary," he began, his voice tinged with a touch of trepidation, "to embark upon a query that may be deemed unduly forward." His words trailed off, his hands fidgeting nervously with his handkerchief.

To her credit, Mary maintained an air of composure, displaying no hint of discomposure at the delicate inquiry. "Indeed, Mr Collins, you may pose your question," replied she, her voice laced with a serene amusement. "Should your inquiry stray beyond the boundaries of propriety, you shall be duly apprised."

Collins swallowed audibly, his anxious gaze fixed upon Mary. "It has not escaped my notice, dear Cousin," he ventured, "that you bear a remarkable resemblance to Miss de Bourgh. And it has made me wonder..." His words trailed off, and he anxiously twisted his handkerchief between his perspiring hands.

Undeterred by the implied audacity of Collins's observation, Mary maintained her poise. "Indeed, the striking resemblance has been noted by many," she replied with serene dignity. "Rest assured, Cousin, it is but a fortuitous coincidence. We possess no connection to the esteemed de Bourgh lineage that we are aware of. Surely, had such a significant bond existed, we would have been privy to the knowledge."

Elizabeth mused silently, her thoughts drifting to the formidable Lady Catherine. Even in this remote corner of Hertfordshire, her influence over Mr Collins remained palpable, a testament to her commanding presence.

Observing her cousin's hands trembling around the fabric of his handkerchief, Lizzy shifted her attention back to the basket, seeking solace in its enigmatic contents.

The clergyman continued speaking, his voice shaking with a combination of respect and fear. "Forgive me, dear Cousin, for the audacity of my next words," he stammered. "But it is my humble observation that while the unfortunate Miss de Bourgh languishes in the clutches of ill health, you embody all the qualities she could possess was she blessed with robust vitality. I confess, my admiration—nay, more than mere admiration!—compels me to acknowledge that if you were to grace me with your favour and accept my advances, Lady Catherine would be grievously offended to see me return with a wife bearing such a resemblance to her ailing daughter."

Elizabeth's mouth fell agape, aghast at her cousin's brazenness. Did he not comprehend the impropriety of his words in their current company?

Aware of the breach in etiquette, Mary blushed, her gaze falling demurely to her plain sewing. "Sir, your generous appraisal far exceeds what is proper," she responded with a hint of modesty. "I am genuinely flattered by your... consideration, but it is premature to entertain such decisive measures at present."

The transformative effect her influence had on Mr Collins became apparent, for he bowed in acquiescence. "As you wish, dear Cousin," he conceded, putting the matter to rest.

Elizabeth could not deny that with his complexion clearing and his hair neatly groomed, Mr Collins possessed a certain charm, far more amiable than his initial impression had suggested. Free from the incessant comparisons to Lady Catherine, he appeared quite likeable indeed.

Ever eager to share news of social engagements, Catherine interjected, "Lizzy, you were absent when Charlotte visited. The

Lucases are hosting a ball and extending invitations also to the officers. We have all made suitable preparations, but it seems you have not acquired a new gown since Mary's first Season."

The mere thought of dancing and merriment stirred a pang of unease within Elizabeth's heart. "Oh, Kitty, I implore you, not now," pleaded she, a shiver coursing through her. "I... require some time before I can contemplate such festivities without discomfort."

As her words hung in the air, Lizzy felt both relief and apprehension settling upon her. She had successfully diverted the conversation away from her clandestine activities, yet the weight of her hidden actions bore heavily upon her conscience. The basket concealed a dark secret known only to her while her sisters and Mr Collins remained blissfully unaware.

They all fell into a hushed silence, punctuated only by the faint rustling of skirts and the birds teetering from outside the opened window.

*∧*∧*

"Good heavens!" Bingley exclaimed, placing the note on the table before him, then picking it up again as if unable to fathom the words inscribed within.

Darcy arched an eyebrow inquisitively. "Pray, may I inquire as to the cause of such distress?"

With a trembling hand, Bingley passed the note to his companion. Before Darcy could finish reading half of its contents, he comprehended the source of his friend's dismay. "Naturally, you shall notify your servants and tenants without delay?"

"Indeed," Bingley replied, his voice lacking its usual composure. "What a dreadful occurrence."

Darcy could not dispute the gravity of the situation. Only the most cowardly and debased of men would perpetrate such an attack. The rumours circulating about such vile acts, condoned by certain factions in the name of honour, did nothing to mitigate their repugnance. Bennet's response was fitting: whoever was responsible must face justice promptly. Darcy himself would have taken the same course of action had one of his tenants suffered a similar fate.

"If you have no objections, I shall bring this matter to my cousin's attention," declared Darcy. "Unfortunately, given the recent arrival of the militia, suspicions shall inevitably fall upon them. It is best to commence the investigation there as expeditiously as possible."

Bingley nodded in agreement. "I suggest you arm yourself if any encounter impedes your progress. If one were to chance upon this fiend while he perpetrates his abominable acts..."

"Indeed, I am resolved to do so," he assured Bingley. The lamentable truth resided in the fact that individuals with deviant inclinations could be found across all strata of society. In the bustling city, these so-called "gentlemen" might even sponsor establishments masquerading as "charitable institutions" for orphaned children. However fervently he desired to eradicate such perversions, he recognised the limits of his influence, restricted to safeguarding those within his sphere to the utmost of his abilities.

He strode purposefully through the grand entrance, only to encounter Fitzwilliam dismounting his steed, his countenance holding a grave expression.

Darcy proffered the missive to Fitzwilliam, and his cousin nodded in affirmation. "Meryton is abuzz with the discourse. The amiable townsfolk firmly believe that the officers fail in maintaining proper discipline among their ranks."

"I had anticipated as much." Darcy released a sigh, burdened by his apprehensions. "I presume the authorities have commenced their investigations?"

"Forster has initiated inquiries," Fitzwilliam confirmed with a grimace. "Yet, I fear they shall yield trifling results. It is apparent that this man has received undue promotion courtesy of his uncle, General Williams. Oh, and I have received this missive." From his saddlebag, he produced a letter and extended it to Darcy.

Darcy's brows ascended as he perused the contents of the epistle. Moments later, he recoiled in alarm. "They have divulged this information to Aunt Catherine?"

"You need not be concerned." The Colonel shook his head. "It falls upon me to bring her here, embroiled in this 'foolish undertaking'." He expertly mimicked their aunt's acerbic manner, compelling Darcy to suppress a smile.

"She will bring Anne," Darcy pointed out. "Afterward, she will disseminate our purported engagement to anyone willing to listen, thereby coercing me to wed my 'intended'."

Fitzwilliam grinned impishly. "Come now, Darcy, there are certain advantages. Imagine how swiftly Miss Bingley will redirect her attention from you to my brother."

A most undignified snort escaped Darcy's control. "Indeed, Randall would likely find her company quite captivating." He shook his head ruefully. "However... did they offer no explanation for their collective arrival at this juncture?"

"Not a word," the Colonel replied nonchalantly. "Undoubtedly, the truth shall unveil itself ere long." He cast an appraising gaze upon Netherfield. "While it may adequately accommodate Aunt Catherine, I surmise the remainder of the family will deem this locale most congenial. It would be prudent to forewarn Bingley of his impending guests, for no other dwelling can accommodate them."

"And what of you?" Darcy inquired, unenthusiastic about adding more unfavourable—nay, awkward—tidings to Bingley's already beleaguered day.

Fitzwilliam's mirth swiftly evaporated. "I shall engage in a tête-à-tête with our old acquaintance."

The Colonel felt a sense of disdain as he had observed Wickham's unchanged demeanour throughout the years. That cheerful and amiable facade, so effortlessly donned in social gatherings, could easily inspire trust in unsuspecting souls, only to be betrayed without a second thought. In a span of fewer than seven days, Wickham had managed to accumulate significant gambling debts among Meryton's most esteemed circles. It was in the dreariest tavern of Meryton that Fitzwilliam had stumbled upon him, accompanied by a group of young officers. Colonel Forster would certainly not relish their forthcoming encounter.

*∧*∧*

Nodding at Wickham, the Colonel motioned towards a seat. "Pray, take a seat."

Fitzwilliam had been fortunate enough to receive a private parlour, graciously offered by the innkeeper of Meryton's finest establishment, which had proven invaluable in conducting such interviews.

Wickham seated himself, sporting a cheerfully insolent smile. "I am grateful, sir. How may I be of service to you?"

Fitzwilliam could have happily rearranged a few of Wickham's teeth at that moment. To witness him so calmly when he had nearly ruined Darcy's sister! Georgiana had fallen under the spell of that callous rogue, convinced she was in love and had almost eloped. Wickham's complete absence of remorse merely accentuated his utter lack of decency.

Rather than allowing his anger to gain the upper hand, the Colonel spoke with measured composure. "Considering the company you keep, it is quite possible that you have been privy to more than the ordinary gossip concerning the girl discovered this morning."

Wickham appeared unconcerned. "As I have heard it, it is but the trouble caused by some farmer's offspring, sir," responded he nonchalantly. "Surely, it is hardly a matter that would concern a gentleman of your standing."

Fitzwilliam retorted coolly, suppressing any outward display of anger, "I surmise that those responsible would prefer others to perceive it in such a light." The townsfolk held a different view, attributing blame to the militia. "I am resolved to bring this matter to a satisfactory resolution."

Wickham's response was a slow blink, betraying his subtle change of expression. "And here I thought you had come to accuse me of such an act."

"I advise you to reconsider the audacity of your comment." The Colonel would have relished the opportunity to act upon Wickham's suggestion. Numerous young women would deem it a fitting retribution for his transgressions. "Your proposition is far too tempting."

A grin played upon Wickham's lips. "Ah, but you, Colonel, are a man of honour."

"And you, sir, find yourself indebted to individuals who would gladly shatter every bone in your body should you fail to settle your dues." Fitzwilliam knew the type well, having encountered Wickham's aftermath on more than one occasion, just as his cousin had. "Should you persist in being difficult, I may very well choose to leave you to your fate."

Wickham's smile remained unyielding. "Poor Georgie. It would be most unfortunate if our correspondence were to come to light."

The Colonel regarded the man with his most frigid stare. "Indeed, it would. A certain young man by the name of Wickham might soon find himself demoted and dispatched to the front lines of the Peninsula." The notion penetrated Wickham's smug veneer, and Richard continued, "As the orders of war have not been rescinded, any militiaman is susceptible to transfer into the regular forces."

Wickham swallowed hard, the possibility of such a fate evidently not having crossed his mind when he had purchased his commission. The realisation of his precarious situation began to chip away at his smugness.

Fitzwilliam maintained his unwavering gaze; his voice laced with a subtle warning. "Think carefully, Mr Wickham. A man of your reputation and connections would surely find the harsh realities of the battlefield far less accommodating than the indulgent confines of Meryton society."

A flicker of unease passed through Wickham's eyes, a crack in his self-assured facade. The weight of the consequences finally seemed to settle upon him. "Colonel, I assure you that any misunderstanding is regrettable, and I am more than willing to cooperate in resolving this matter."

Fitzwilliam inclined his head slightly, acknowledging the shift in Wickham's tone. "Cooperation, indeed. It would be in your best interest to provide any information that might assist in identifying the true culprits responsible for the girl's predicament. Rest assured, I am not here to accuse you but to seek the truth."

Wickham nodded, his demeanour now considerably more subdued. "I shall endeavour to aid your investigation, Colonel. Though I must confess that my knowledge of the incident is limited, I may be able to shed some light on the activities of certain individuals who might be involved."

Fitzwilliam's stern countenance softened ever so slightly, a glimmer of cautious optimism in his eyes. "Very well, Mr Wickham. Your willingness to cooperate is commendable. I shall expect your full cooperation in this endeavour. Lives and reputations hang in the balance."

With that, Wickham rose from his seat, a sense of newfound responsibility replacing his previous insolence. "You have my word, Colonel. I shall do everything within my power to assist you in uncovering the truth."

Fitzwilliam regarded him gravely, his voice laden with caution and authority. "See that you do, Mr Wickham. For your own sake and for the sake of those who have been wronged."

As Wickham departed the private parlour, Fitzwilliam was left to contemplate the tangled web of deceit and betrayal that had woven itself around Meryton. The search for justice would require both astuteness and discretion, for the revelations that lay ahead had the potential to upend the delicate equilibrium of their society.

With an unwavering determination, Colonel Fitzwilliam prepared to navigate the treacherous path before him, vowing to protect the innocent and expose the guilty, regardless of the consequences. In this intricate dance of shadows and secrets, he would endeavour to restore order and bring a resolution befitting the principles of honour and integrity he held dear.

# Chapter 6

In a twist of fate, Darcy found himself eagerly anticipating an upcoming ball, a sensation hitherto foreign to his discerning nature. This newfound enthusiasm had little to do with the charms of the provincial Lucas family or the congeniality of their house, Lucas Lodge, which paled in comparison to the modest Longbourn estate. Instead, Darcy's eagerness stemmed from the prospect of momentarily escaping the burdensome tension that had plagued his days and revel in the fleeting freedom the ball would afford. Alas, his respite would be short-lived, as the following day would witness the grand arrival of the Fitzwilliam family at Netherfield, accompanied by his formidable aunt and meek cousin.

Lady Catherine, true to form, had asserted herself as the one descending while her brother's family trailed dutifully in her wake. This arrangement did little to uplift Darcy's spirits; indeed, the prospect of her arrival resembled a man facing his own execution.

To make matters worse, another young girl, the daughter of a labourer from Meryton, fell victim to the same fate as the tenant farmer's child. Colonel Fitzwilliam, having overruled Colonel Forster, found himself compelled to confine the entire militia to camp until the whereabouts of each man on the nights of the attacks could be verified. Without such precautionary measures, the death of the first victim would likely have been followed by the townsfolk seeking retribution against one or more soldiers.

Privately, Darcy harboured suspicions that Fitzwilliam longed for the respite from the arduous task of sorting through records and statements that the ball would provide. By virtue of a card party held on the night of the second attack, he had managed to parole nearly half of the officers, and many enlisted men had verifiable alibis from their time spent in camp. However, it came as no surprise to Darcy that Lieutenant Wickham was amongst those whose whereabouts could not be fully accounted for. Though Wickham had attended the card party, three of the Miss Bennets had observed his absence during a portion of the evening, a fact corroborated by several other witnesses, including some of Wickham's fellow officers.

Darcy sighed, silently wishing that Fitzwilliam were present to shield him from Miss Bingley's persistent attentions. It was undoubtedly selfish and unfair to entertain such thoughts, however. After all, Caroline Bingley epitomised the typical example of society, and as such, she could hardly be faulted for conforming to societal expectations. Women as delightfully unconventional as Miss Elizabeth Bennet were exceedingly rare. Not only did she possess extraordinary accomplishments, but she also refrained from asserting any superiority over her peers.

This unique combination intrigued Darcy. In Miss Elizabeth's presence, he felt an awakening akin to an ageing steed flexing long-neglected muscles to outpace a newfound challenger. Such a realisation led him to question how much he had forsaken when he retreated to Pemberley following his father's demise. Immersed in the management of his estate and harbouring disdain for society, he had done himself a disservice by neglecting to seek out kindred spirits as friends.

If it were not for Bingley's persistent insistence, Darcy might never have formed a friendship with the younger man or embarked on the journey to Hertfordshire. The notion that his increasing isolation might have deprived him of his acquaintance with Miss Elizabeth served as a prod, compelling him to embrace a newfound openness, unlike anything he had previously exhibited.

*∧*∧*

With its rambling and eclectic architecture, Lucas Lodge boasted sections that dated back to the Elizabethan era, supplemented by more recent additions that seemed haphazardly appended. Despite its age and eccentric modifications, the estate provided a comfortable abode, complete with an ancient great hall adorned with lofty ceilings and imposing oak beams, a testament to its rich history.

Under different circumstances, Lizzy would have delighted to attend the ball. However, with the distressing attacks on innocent young girls weighing heavily on her mind, she found herself incapable of engaging in the customary banter and pleasantries orchestrated by Sir William.

The man, to his credit, had displayed genuine concern for the victims of the attacks, being amongst the first to extend assistance to the afflicted families. Yet, having fulfilled his obligations and taken necessary precautions with his tenants and servants, he promptly dismissed the matter from his thoughts and resumed his cheerful and affable demeanour, extending his warmth to individuals of every rank and station.

Elizabeth cast a longing gaze towards her father, who had sought solace in the library of Sir William's home, where he would likely remain until the ball's conclusion. Oh, how she envied his retreat from the impending social obligations. Alas, she had no such sanctuary.

*∧*∧*

"Miss Elizabeth, might I have the pleasure of the ensuing dance?" inquired Mr Darcy as he gazed upon her, though her smile appeared somewhat contrived in her own perception.

"I would be most honoured, sir, though I fear I cannot vouch for avoiding unsuitable discourse."

Darcy returned her smile, yet his eyes betrayed an air of apprehension. "A lady of your quality can render any subject appropriate. Even—" His smile broadened, and a flicker of amusement ignited in his eyes. "Animal husbandry, perhaps." He extended his hand.

Elizabeth accepted the gesture and accompanied Darcy to join the forming sets. "Or perhaps even Sappho?"

"Indeed, even so." A measure of tension relinquished its hold on Darcy's countenance. "A true lady possesses the power to bestow respectability upon the most disreputable of Greeks."

As the music commenced, he executed a bow in response to her curtsey.

Lizzy found herself warming to the verbal sparring. "How truly extraordinary, sir. I had been under the impression that the ancient Greeks maintained practices beyond the confines of respectability."

"They did possess a certain indiscriminateness," conceded Darcy.

Their movements in the dance momentarily separated them, and upon reuniting, Elizabeth remarked archly, "You are far too magnanimous, Mr Darcy."

He regarded her with a grave expression. "In the presence of an inspiration such as yourself, how could I not be?"

A blush suffused her face. She considered herself neither generous nor inspiring. "Ah, I perceive your intention to unsettle me with extravagant praise."

"I assure you, I proffer praise solely where it is merited."

Elizabeth's countenance glowed with a vivid hue. "Are you quite certain that your account has been accurately tallied, sir? The sum owed seems exorbitant."

"I believe it has been calculated with the utmost carelessness," retorted Darcy, his countenance a mask of seriousness.

Lizzy feigned astonishment. "Alas, my honour has thus been impugned."

*∧*∧*

Fitzwilliam began to ease his anxieties upon realising that several officers, who had not been cleared of wrongdoing, were present at the ball. He struggled immensely to complete the dance without causing offence to his partner.

Forster's explanation for their presence did nothing to assuage Fitzwilliam's state of mind. It was intolerable to allow men under investigation to attend a ball simply because their more fortunate comrades were in attendance.

Darcy joined him in the secluded corner of Lucas Lodge's grand room. "What on earth is that scoundrel doing here?"

Fitzwilliam sighed. "Forster deems it unjust to confine the officers who have not yet been cleared to the confines of the camp."

"What?"

The Colonel met his cousin's stern gaze with composure. "Indeed. At this juncture, our best course of action is to keep a vigilant eye on the men in question and hope that no further attack occurs." He shook his head when Darcy made a half-hearted gesture towards a sword or pistol that he did not possess. "No duels, my dear cousin. They shall achieve nothing."

"So we merely observe?"

"Come now, Darcy. You shall give yourself a frightful headache." Fitzwilliam motioned for silence. "Several of the cleared men bear ill will towards some of those under doubt. I shall engage them in conversation throughout the evening." The

Colonel understood that such measures were insufficient, but they constituted the extent of his available options. "Go forth and partake in a dance with your Miss Elizabeth."

"She is not 'my' Miss Elizabeth," Darcy retorted through clenched teeth.

Years of military life had taught Fitzwilliam the value of seizing moments of enjoyment whenever they presented themselves. He chuckled at his cousin's discomfort. "The way she brightens when you engage her? Oh, I do believe she is very much yours, cousin."

Darcy's blush proved to be quite entertaining.

"Come now, Darcy. You must not allow that scoundrel to rob you of your pleasure." Fitzwilliam gently nudged his cousin towards Miss Bennets. If anyone deserved happiness, it was Darcy.

*∧*∧*

The tumult that ensued within the confines of Longbourn was an inescapable consequence of five vivacious young women dwelling under the same roof. While the affairs of the household continued to transpire smoothly, Mr Bennet found himself even more frequently compelled to seek solace in his library, simply to evade the overpowering aura of femininity that pervaded the premises. The lively discussions that ensued in the wake of the recent ball hosted by the Lucas family, particularly centring on the joys inherent in an abundance of young gentlemen, ensuring that no damsel was coerced into relinquishing a dance, were more than sufficient to drive him towards his preferred retreat. It was a place where the discourse of youthful beaus and merriment on the dance floor was strictly forbidden.

While he was hiding in his sanctuary and Mrs Bennet was yet to return from her visit to Waters, it fell upon Elizabeth, whom the flustered servant was able to locate, to ascertain that

Longbourn had been infiltrated by grand carriages and noble gentlemen who accompanied Mr Darcy. A furtive glance through the draperies of the front parlour served to validate the servant's agitated assessment. Not less than three carriages stood adjacent to the estate, with gallant gentlemen lending their aid to unfamiliar ladies whom Lizzy had not hitherto encountered.

Though her mind pondered the impetus that had impelled Mr Darcy and his cousin Colonel Fitzwilliam to impose such an extraordinary assemblage upon their modest abode, Elizabeth speedily cast aside such contemplation in favour of directing the preparation of a light tea for their unanticipated guests to be served upon the finest china. Furthermore, she took charge of ushering their visitors into the front parlour, the sole room in Longbourn equipped to accommodate so sizable a company.

Alas, there was scarce time to transform their attire from the day dresses they currently wore into more befitting garments for receiving visitors. In truth, there was scarcely enough time for her sisters to relocate themselves from the southern parlour to the dimmer and chillier front parlour. Extracting their father from the library proved as arduous an endeavour as she had anticipated. Although Lizzy possessed the capacity to receive guests with the utmost composure, she perceived no reason to impress upon their visitors how exceedingly atypical the Bennet household could be. Fortunately for Elizabeth, Mrs Bennet had returned and compelled her husband to be present in the parlour in a matter of seconds.

The introductions that ensued proved no less astonishing. The Bennets found themselves murmuring polite salutations to what appeared to be the entire extended family of Mr Darcy. Save for his conspicuously absent sister, the residence of Longbourn had been infiltrated by the Earl of Ashton, accompanied by his wife, Lady Ashton, their two sons, Lord Fitzwilliam and Colonel Fitzwilliam, as well as Lady Catherine de Bourgh and her daughter Anne, who indeed bore a striking resemblance to Mary, arousing much consternation.

Once their esteemed guests were seated within the confines of the front parlour, Mrs Bennet voiced her sentiments, saying, "While I express my honour in the face of such an illustrious gathering, I confess myself equally perplexed as to its purpose."

The Earl turned his gaze from the lady to her daughter, Miss Mary, then his niece, Anne. "Can you not surmise, Madam?"

Had Elizabeth found herself alone, she would have winced upon witnessing her father's response.

"The resemblance is striking," said he, "but surely it is a mere coincidence."

"That, sir, is precisely what we have convened here to ascertain," asserted the Earl with an underlying resolve that belied his amiable countenance. A gentleman much older than Mr Bennet exuded an air of determination that brooked no opposition on this matter.

Lady Catherine's eyes narrowed in a display of haughty scepticism. "There can be no conceivable connection," declared she with conviction. "That young upstart," she gestured dismissively towards Mary, "bears no resemblance whatsoever to Anne."

Miss de Bourgh, however, did not flinch; instead, she seemed to shrink further into her chair, her countenance as pallid as the morning mist. Elizabeth feared that she might succumb to a fainting spell.

Mary's face flushed with indignation and ire, though she chose her words with remarkable restraint. "We would never presume to besmirch the reputation of one of your esteemed standing by insinuating any connection, your ladyship," stated the girl, her voice laced with quiet dignity.

The gentlemen in the room discreetly coughed, and while Mrs Bennet was shaking her head at Mary's impertinence, an unmistakable glimmer of amusement danced in Mr Bennet's eyes as if he had long anticipated the clash of such formidable personalities.

The Earl cleared his throat delicately, addressing Mr Bennet with a raised eyebrow. "Your previous wife, the late Mrs Bennet, was a Miss Gardiner if I am not mistaken?"

Lady Catherine, sitting stiffly in her chair, drew in a sharp breath.

Mr Bennet, looking slightly bewildered by the unexpected question, nodded in agreement. " Miss Janet Gardiner, though she was Jannie to everyone."

"The sister of Miss Cassandra Gardiner and Mr Edward Gardiner, I presume?" The Earl's eyes twinkled with a hint of mischief.

Again, Mr Bennet nodded.

"Then, my dear sir, we have a predicament," the Earl sighed, spreading his hands in a gesture of apparent helplessness. "You see, twenty-five years ago, my sister Catherine's daughter Janet and her governess, Mrs Gardiner, disappeared without a trace. And, as it so happens, Mrs Gardiner had two children, a daughter Cassandra who was then fourteen, and a son Edward, who was not yet five."

Lizzy watched in awe as Lady Catherine, visibly shaken, struggled to maintain her composure.

Mary, ever the dutiful sister, rushed to Miss de Bourgh's side to offer assistance, as the latter seemed in a similar state to that of her mother.

"Impossible!" cried Lady Catherine in a tone that brooked no argument. "My Janet died. She did not disappear!"

Her tirade continued at length, vehemently insisting on the impossibility of any connection with the Bennets, repeatedly emphasising their obvious inferiority.

Mr Bennet, usually so quick-witted, was at a loss for words.

The Earl, for his part, remained unflappable in the face of Lady Catherine's outburst. "The decision, my dear sister, is not yours to make," said he in a dry voice. "Sir Lewis's will is quite clear on the matter. Rosings Park is left to his daughter Janet if she still lives, or to her heirs, and only then, to Anne."

Lady Catherine paled visibly at the mention of her daughter's inheritance. "You shall not steal Anne's birthright!" cried she.

Her ladyship seemed oblivious to the fact that her daughter had slipped out of the room with Mary only moments earlier. It was no wonder poor Miss de Bourgh appeared so frail and unwell with such a mother.

"Speaking of which, where is Anne?" Lord Fitzwilliam's question hung in the air.

Lady Catherine's hand went to her chest as though she had been physically struck.

Elizabeth knew it was time to intervene before another outburst could occur. "Miss de Bourgh was looking quite unwell, so my sister Mary helped her from the room," she interjected, her tone polite but firm. "Shall I see where they have gone?"

Lady Catherine's expression was pure venom, but the other members of the Darcy family looked visibly relieved and grateful. Lizzy curtsied gracefully and made her exit, reflecting on the strange turn of events. It was no wonder poor Mr Collins was so intimidated by his patroness. Lady Catherine was the kind of harridan who would terrorise anyone, even the Prince Regent himself.

*∧*∧*

As anticipated by Elizabeth, Mary had escorted Miss de Bourgh to the south parlour. The young women engaged in lively conversation, and the serene ambience of the warmer chamber seemed to have a positive effect on Anne's disposition.

"Miss de Bourgh?"

The young lady recoiled within herself.

Elizabeth endeavoured to bestow a reassuring smile. "Might I convey to your family that you are in good health and contented in this tranquil place, thus sparing you any disruption?"

She winced at the clamorous voices emanating from the front parlour, then offered a sardonic twist of her lips. "That would be most welcome. Mama can be... overpowering."

"Undoubtedly," responded Elizabeth in a wry tone. "Rest assured, Miss de Bourgh, neither my sisters nor I harbour any desire to deprive you of your inheritance, even if a connection exists as your uncle perceives."

Miss de Bourgh shook her head. "Pray, call me Anne. Should a connection indeed exist, we would be closely related."

"Then you must address me as Lizzy," Elizabeth added with a smile. "Though, I fear I could not bring myself to call you Aunt, even if such a connection were established."

Anne, who appeared to Lizzy to be in her late twenties, smiled, her countenance regaining its colour. "Oh, that would be utterly absurd. I could not fathom being an aunt to five young ladies; it is positively reminiscent of a spinster's fate."

Mary chuckled softly. "Indubitably. We, as young ladies, must shun any appearance of spinsterhood, lest it becomes our unalterable reality."

Meanwhile, in the parlour, except for Lady Catherine, all of Longbourn's distinguished guests breathed a sigh of relief upon hearing Elizabeth's account of Miss Anne de Bourgh's comfortable repose in the south parlour.

Lady Catherine displayed some discontent. "Is it to be tolerated that my daughter should endure such inferior conditions?" she glared at her brother. "I fail to comprehend why poor Anne must endure this ordeal."

A heavy sigh escaped the Earl's lips. "No, Catherine. It is not a matter of comprehension. Rather, you refuse to acknowledge that Anne, not yourself, holds the position of authority at Rosings Park and, furthermore, that Miss Bennet may rightfully claim ownership."

Jane blushed and cast her eyes downward. "I harbour no desire to dispossess anyone of their home."

Elizabeth found herself unsure whether to bless or condemn Mrs Hill, who, with the utmost discretion, opened the door and whispered to Mrs Bennet, "Pardon me, ma'am, but Mrs Phillips has arrived."

Lizzy's aunt was undoubtedly a distraction, yet she might possess some insight into what appeared to Elizabeth as a futile dispute. However, why had she come, and why now?

A partial answer to that query manifested itself in the glances exchanged between the Colonel and Mr Darcy, both of whom found Lady Catherine's vehement denial of any connection between the Bennets and herself profoundly amusing.

"Bring Mrs Phillips here," murmured Mrs Bennet. She refrained from mentioning that the addition of one more highly-strung individual could hardly exacerbate the situation.

Lizzy looked at her mother's countenance and half-anticipated her to employ her most efficacious remedy for hysteria: a swift slap across the face of the afflicted party. Should that prove fruitless, a splash of cold water on the countenance typically succeeded.

The whispered conference between three cousins did little to assuage Elizabeth's agitation. The entire affair was utterly preposterous. Had her birth mother possessed any other family but that of a moderately prosperous widow, should she have informed her husband of such matters?

The parlour door swung open once more, ushering in the arrival of Mrs Phillips, who entered the room with an air of trepidation akin to facing her darkest fears. Her countenance, drained of all colour, froze in a petrified state as her eyes surveyed the parlour's surroundings.

Though her lips made several valiant attempts to form

words, it became apparent that the woman was incapable of coaxing any sound from her trembling mouth.

With a venomous breath intake, Lady Catherine hissed forth her indignation. "You! Ungrateful wench! You and your thieving mother ought to have been banished from society."

Flushed with a mixture of embarrassment and defiance, Mrs Phillips stood taller and addressed the noble lady. "My dear mother took nought, madam. It was all the product of Jannie's deranged imaginings."

As Elizabeth struggled to gather her thoughts amidst the mounting tension, Lady Catherine found herself gaping in utter disbelief at the audacity of being contradicted. Meanwhile, the Earl, unable to contain his curiosity, ventured forth with a query. "Is this tale to be believed, then? Jannie Gardiner was truly none other than Janet de Bourgh?"

Mrs Phillips, her head nodding in affirmation, responded with a voice strained and peculiarly taut. "Indeed, it was Jannie who orchestrated this entire affair," uttered she, her words hanging in the air with an extraordinary weight. "She held an intense loathing for both Rosings and her mother." Having made this astounding revelation, Mrs Phillips suddenly faltered, her body swaying unsteadily before succumbing to the depths of unconsciousness.

# Chapter 7

Darcy had started to anticipate some affiliation between the Bennets and the de Bourghs, even if solely due to his aunt's vehement denial that any such association could exist; however, he was not prepared for such a sensational confirmation. He half-ascended, with the intention of offering assistance to Mrs Phillips, only to retract when that respectable lady was engulfed by her nieces. Aunt Catherine's clamorous protestations merely served to pound a throbbing ache into his head.

Fitzwilliam caught his gaze and contorted his countenance into a wry expression.

Darcy shook his head at his cousin. At least Anne was spared from this madness. It would be detrimental for her to witness her mother screeching like a harpy, proclaiming that Mrs Phillips must be a degenerate liar for daring to suggest that her Janet would engage in such a disrespectful act.

He blinked in astonishment as Mrs Bennet stood and strode purposefully toward Lady Catherine, administering two resounding slaps, one on each cheek.

For a prolonged—blissfully quiet—interval, her ladyship was rendered speechless by this assault.

Mrs Bennet inclined her head towards the startled Earl. "Your lordship, I find a sharp shock typically suffices to pacify a bout of hysteria. The lady should consume a small measure of brandy to calm her nerves."

Darcy bit his lips, suppressing a smile, particularly since his uncle was struggling to maintain a composed countenance.

"I am grateful, madam," replied he, his voice only slightly unsteady. "Would you be so kind as to make the arrangements? I defer to your wisdom in this regard."

Mrs Bennet curtsied and withdrew to the door, where Darcy suspected a gathering of servants stood in anticipation, eavesdropping. If he were candid with himself, he would have preferred to join them at the door, thereby avoiding witnessing his aunt's madness.

Lady Catherine finally regained her voice. "How... how can this..."

To Darcy's surprise, his Aunt Eleanor responded calmly, albeit with a steely edge in her tone. "My dear sister, you were overcome with emotion. Do endeavour to remain composed until the brandy is brought to you."

Perhaps it was the shock of witnessing gentle and serene Lady Eleanor approving of such treatment that caused Lady Catherine to subside. In any case, she had not found her voice until the indomitable Mrs Bennet returned with the brandy.

"Sip it slowly, your ladyship. It shall calm your nerves." Though the woman's tone remained respectful, Darcy could not shake the disconcerting impression that she derived a degree of inappropriate amusement from the situation.

Undoubtedly, her presence was sufficient to keep Lady Catherine quiet and—astonishingly—compliant.

Darcy doubted Mrs Phillips fared any better. Awaking to a flock of Bennet girls and their genuine concern must have starkly contrasted with Darcy's family's inquisitive and not entirely benevolent gazes.

The Earl offered a slight bow. "I offer my sincere apologies, madam. I had not intended to cause such a shock."

Mrs Phillips once assisted to a chair, could only blink in

response.

He continued as though oblivious to her reaction. "Please, do not fret that you shall suffer the consequences of others' actions. You were not of an age to fully comprehend the situation, and if Janet convinced your mother, then no blame can be attributed to her either. We seek only the truth."

Brandy was proffered to Mrs Phillips to assuage her agitated nerves – a remedy Mr Darcy found far more palatable than the customary smelling salts.

The Earl patiently waited until her breathing regained a modicum of composure before inquiring with a genteel solicitude, "Might I entreat upon your kindness to recount what you know of Janet's departure from Rosings and her subsequent life?"

Mrs Phillips blinked, then swallowed, her countenance betraying a distinct lack of solace in the presence of her nieces' well-meaning attentions.

"She... insisted we address her as Jannie whenever her mother was absent," Mrs Phillips finally divulged, taking a swallow of gold liquor. "Her joy knew no bounds when surrounded by a throng of people." Another gulp. "Our mother indulged her to the utmost – at times, I dare say Mama cared more for her than for the rest of us." Another gulp. "Jannie adored her father, but Sir Lewis was frequently occupied with business, and Jannie contended that her mother's sternness had stifled her spirit, leaving no room for the exuberance befitting a sixteen-year-old longing for emancipation."

Lady Catherine began to interject but chose to take another sip of brandy instead, prompted by a gesture from Mrs Bennet.

"That was when Mama's brother in Meryton passed away, bequeathing everything to her. It was not an extravagant fortune but included a townhouse and enough for Mama to live comfortably while affording me a respectable dowry without jeopardising Edward's prospects." Mrs Phillips shut her eyes.

"Yet Jannie insisted on accompanying us. I cannot fathom—She wanted to be Miss Jannie Gardiner, loved by everyone, rather than Miss Janet de Bourgh, hated by her own mother. She brought along some of her jewellery – sufficient to be sold, thus furnishing her with a dowry comparable to mine, ensuring that no one would suspect her true ancestry."

Mr Bennet appeared as if he had ingested a live amphibian. "Why did she never confide in me?" inquired he softly, seemingly not expecting a response.

Yet a response he received. "Jannie feared you would insist upon contacting the de Bourghs had she disclosed it, brother," Mrs Phillips answered. "Her sole remorse lay in her inability to bear you a son."

Mr Bennet turned his head, dabbing at his eyes. He seemed much older, burdened by the weight of sorrow. "My poor Jannie." His utterance was clearly not intended for public ears.

Mrs Phillips, thankfully, possessed the discernment to disregard the remark. "Mama attempted to reject her presence, but Jannie disguised herself as one of the carriage drivers, and by the time we discovered the ruse, it was too late. She could not return unaccompanied, and she professed that her mother would disown her. Mama's tender heart could not bear to send her away, and therefore, upon our arrival in Meryton, Jannie became an integral part of Mama's household, just as she had intended."

Mrs Phillips let out a wistful sigh. "There is little more to divulge thereafter. Jannie wed Mr Bennet, and I entered into matrimony with Mr Phillips. She divulged her secret to no one, not even Edward, who was too young to retain any recollection of those events. And when she departed this world, she was laid to rest as Jannie Bennet, née Gardiner. I still yearn for her presence." With that, Mrs Phillips's eyelids closed, and another sigh escaped her lips.

After such an extraordinary confession, a prolonged silence

enveloped the gathering.

Mrs Phillips had imbibed a sufficient amount of brandy to attain a notable state of relaxation, making her even more effusive. Thus, she suddenly spoke again. "There was, in fact, a reason behind Jannie's actions," proclaimed she, once again capturing the attention of the entire room. "She always believed that her mother had harboured no affection for her. However, it was when she turned fifteen that she discovered the truth. At that time, her aunt, Lady Anne, graced Rosings with her presence, and under the influence of a few glasses of brandy, Lady Catherine unburdened herself to her sister, revealing a secret that she had been concealing for so long. Unbeknownst to the ladies, Jannie happened to be in the next room and overheard everything."

The room suddenly resounded with the sound of rapid movements as Lady Catherine attempted to rise, only to be thwarted by the strong effects of the brandy, causing her head to spin. "You witch!" she shouted, yet said no more as Mrs Bennet's severe look fell upon her.

"Madam, I implore you to proceed," Lord Ashdon addressed Mrs Phillips. "What secret did Janet discover?"

A dramatic pause ensued before Mrs Phillips finally uttered, "Jannie discovered that she had not been Lady Catherine's daughter, but her sister. Furthermore, she learned that her birth mother was none other than her grandmother, Lady Mary."

"Sister?" cried the Viscount, casting astonished glances between his cousin, brother and father. The latter, however, appeared not entirely shocked. "How could this be?"

At this juncture, Lady Catherine imbibed enough brandy to prompt another confession, this time to a larger audience. Keeping the secret for forty years was sufficiently long.

"A widow of Earl Ashdon—" stammered she, "a widow at the age of three and forty giving birth to a child out of wedlock thirteen months after her husband passing? That could not have been borne! Consider the scandal! The disgrace!"

"What did you do?" inquired the Earl.

"Me? I did nothing. It was not I who..." Lady Catherine's words failed to pass her lips. "When Mother arrived at Rosings, she divulged her... *predicament*. I, being unable to provide Lewis with an heir, agreed to the plan she had proposed—she would give birth to the child and present it to me as my own. No one would suspect a thing. And I consented because I could not grant Lewis a child," she sobbed.

Crying Lady Catherine was quite a sight to behold.

"This is preposterous!" burst out Lord Fitzwilliam. "How could such a thing even be possible?" cried he. He struggled to comprehend the tangled web of deceit that now unravelled before him. He turned his gaze to his father, whose face bore the weariness of a man burdened by the weight of hidden truths. "And what of Uncle Lewis?"

"If my memory serves me right, he embarked on a voyage to India around that time," replied the Earl.

Now, all eyes turned to him.

"You were aware of this? " cried the Viscount.

The Earl's eyes met his son's with a mixture of regret and resignation. "Of course not," began he, his voice heavy with emotion. "I did hear whispers, however, but I chose not to give them credence. My own desire to protect the family name from scandal made me choose silence over confrontation with Lady Mary, believing it to be the lesser of two evils. And as nothing came of it, I forgot about it until now. It had been ridiculous even to suspect that Mother and Catherine would have devised such a scheme."

"Even after Lady Mary removed to Rosings and Lady Catherine suddenly became with child?"

"It was not so sudden. Catherine had been trying to give Lewis a child for five years. Her pregnancy was expected, as well as Mother's presence there for that reason."

The room fell into a heavy silence, punctuated only by the muffled sobs of Lady Catherine and the strained breathing of others.

Finally, Fitzwilliam broke the stillness. "Well, Darcy, it appears your observations regarding the familial resemblance were not misguided."

Darcy cleared his throat. "Indeed, it would seem so." He shook his head in disbelief. "I had expected to hear of some tenuous connection, not this. The revelation that Jannie Gardiner was, in fact, Janet de Bourgh, the long-lost heir of Sir Lewis, strains one's credulity."

"And that she was our grandmother's daughter..."

Miss Bennets huddled closely, exchanging hushed words; their animated expressions and gestures were unmistakably indicative of a shared accord. Their unanimity was striking.

"Regrettably, I harboured apprehensions of all of this," the Earl spoke wearily, his voice bearing the weight of fatigue. "And in spite of the later revelation, Janet was still Sir Lewis's rightful heir, declared by law."

Typically serene, Jane exhibited a determination that one could have grown accustomed to observing in Elizabeth. "With due respect, your lordship, we fail to perceive any alteration to the circumstances. Mrs Phillips, though undoubtedly sincere, lacks the substantiation necessary to deprive Miss de Bourgh of her inheritance. Moreover, we have no desire to embroil ourselves in such an endeavour."

Her sisters nodded in concurrence.

The Earl blinked, astonished. "Young lady, you must comprehend the futility of your determination."

"Not so, my lord." Elizabeth leaned forward as if preparing for a contest. "The prevailing knowledge is that Miss Janet de Bourgh met an untimely demise. To resurrect her and assert that Mrs Bennet, formerly Miss Gardiner, was once known as Miss de Bourgh would necessitate an extraordinary assemblage of evidence. Furthermore, it would forever label us as avaricious harridans, driven solely by the pursuit of fortune, having unjustly deprived an innocent young lady of her rightful legacy."

Darcy suppressed laughter that threatened to escape as a cough. "Unfortunately, Uncle, Miss Elizabeth is undeniably correct. Regardless of the quantity of evidence presented, society would invariably perceive Miss Bennets as fortune hunters."

Lord Fitzwilliam mumbled, "To the devil with society."

The Earl remained undeterred. "Young lady, it is explicitly stated in your... uncle's will that your sister Miss Bennet is the legitimate heiress of Rosings Park and the de Bourgh fortune."

"But I am not even his blood," protested Jane.

"But he treated your mother as such. His will was explicit."

Lady Catherine inhaled sharply, emitting a hiss.

Jane's expression hardened. "None of us would harbour the desire to deprive anyone of their rightful home."

Darcy could not help but think that Bingley's absence from this gathering was fortuitous; otherwise, he would surely beseech Miss Bennet for her hand then and there. Such strength concealed within her tranquil and gentle demeanour was an unexpected revelation.

Miss Catherine interjected, "We would be content with being recognised as cousins if need be. That would appease those who ponder the resemblance between Mary and Miss de Bourgh without obliterating anyone's expectations."

The Colonel chuckled. "Were I a wagering man, father, I would place my bets on Miss Bennets. They would give old Boney a moment's pause."

The Earl crossed his arms. "All the more reason to restore what is rightfully theirs." His scowled and no one dared to challenge his assertion.

"Must this matter be decided at present?" Elizabeth

interposed. "This news has been an astonishing blow to many of us gathered here. It might be prudent to take a pause for reflection on the situation." She gestured in Lady Catherine's direction. "I find it difficult to fathom that any of us truly expected news of this nature."

It seemed that Mrs Phillips had consumed an excessive amount of brandy and was unable to respond sensibly. Similarly, Lady Catherine appeared to be affected by the same issue, looking dazed and somewhat drunk. Though Darcy felt guilty for thinking about it, he considered whether it would be possible to make his aunt more amiable by offering her brandy whenever they were together.

# Chapter 8

Whilst the inhabitants of Meryton found themselves in a state of bewilderment, contemplating the sudden arrival of esteemed personages at Netherfield, their concerns were heightened by the distressing news of another unfortunate incident. A young girl of sixteen, the daughter of one of Sir William's tenants, who had been missing for several days, had been found, or rather, her lifeless body.

Meanwhile, at Netherfield, the family of the Earl was confronted with the obstinate refusal of Lady Catherine—now sober—to acknowledge any portion of Mrs Phillips's or her own confession spoken in Longbourn parlour. The rejection echoed with resounding vehemence, displaying an unwavering resolve.

Miss Bennets scoured the halls of Longbourn, endeavouring to unearth evidence pertaining to their birth mother's past. As for Mr Bennet, he sought solace in his library and the indulgence of port, though one could not ascertain which offered him greater allure.

The murmurs circulating in Meryton, alluding to Colonel Fitzwilliam's meticulous examination of every gentleman's attire and his formal petition to the Home Office for the replacement of Colonel Forster, did little to assuage Elizabeth's anxiety.

In fear of succumbing to her already fragile temperament, Lizzy retreated to the attic of Longbourn on the second day of constant rain. Seated amidst the dust, she embarked upon the arduous task of sorting through her deceased mother's trunks, within which lay a few cherished gowns, presumably of sentimental value to her father, several delicately embroidered handkerchiefs, bonnets that now lamentably adhered to an outdated style, and, nestled at the very bottom of the trunk, a weathered, leather-bound book secured by a faded clasp.

Drawing the candle a little nearer, Elizabeth cautiously unfurled the book.

Upon the flyleaf, in a rounded, juvenile script, was inscribed, "The Diary of Janet de Bourgh."

Lizzy's hands trembled. This was incontrovertible evidence, admissible in any court of law. She swallowed hard and, in spite of the meagre illumination, commenced her reading.

"Lizzy?" Catherine's voice intruded upon Elizabeth's reverie. She rubbed her weary eyes and gingerly closed the diary, securing the clasp.

All Aunt Phillips had disclosed was now validated, yet Lizzy felt an unsettling guilt for holding this confirmation within her grasp. How much easier it would have been if this connection remained a mere unsubstantiated anecdote...

"Lizzy?" Kitty's voice carried a note of concern, perhaps even a touch of trepidation. "Are you well?"

"I am quite well, Kitty," replied she, her voice betraying a hint of strain. "I have simply been immersed in my reading for an inordinate length of time."

"Here?" Kitty's voice drew nearer. "You shall impair your eyesight, consuming literature in such dim illumination."

"I had not anticipated reading for such an extended duration," she confessed. "But I stumbled upon Mama's diary."

"Oh," Kitty exhaled softly, barely audible. "Is it an exceedingly... romantic account?"

"It does not resemble the novels wherein the heroine falls

irrevocably in love with the gallant gentleman who rescues her from dire perils," Elizabeth responded, opting for a more elaborate reply instead of a simple affirmation. She supposed that what she regarded as headstrong foolishness, Kitty would undoubtedly perceive as utterly romantic.

"Not that!" Catherine's voice carried a hint of mirth as though she struggled to contain her laughter. "Everyone knows those tales are entirely fabricated and utterly preposterous."

Lizzy rose, wincing as her body protested against the prolonged sitting. She retrieved the candle, its warm glow casting elongated shadows across the attic's timeworn planks. "Mama was but your age when she dared to flee the confines of her home, Kitty," she disclosed, cautiously beginning her descent toward the stairs. "She was fortunate that Grandmama Gardiner chose to embrace her as a daughter."

"So, it is all true, then?" Catherine inquired, a sense of astonishment colouring her words. "Goodness, what an astonishing revelation!"

Lizzy chose to overlook her sister's choice of terminology. The attic staircase, weathered and steep from years of traversing, demanded careful navigation. Maintaining a vigilant gaze and steady footing was prudent when ascending or descending its treacherous steps.

"I must confess, Grandmama Gardiner would be a far more desirable grandmother than Lady Catherine," uttered Catherine, heedless of her sister's disposition. "Grandmama Gardiner was truly amiable."

"Kitty!" Lizzy admonished, but her reprimand carried little weight as she herself entirely concurred with her sister's sentiment. "Such impoliteness is most unbecoming."

Catherine emitted a disdainful sound, lacking in propriety. "Poor Mr Collins, compelled to exhibit civility towards someone of that sort! You should have witnessed his reaction upon learning of her presence. Poor Mary was compelled to devote the entire afternoon to appeasing him."

At the threshold of her chamber, Elizabeth hesitated. Part of her yearned to conceal the diary, preserving Jannie Bennet's secret for a while longer. Yet, her conscience impelled her to share it with her sisters and, perchance, even with Mr Darcy's kin.

"Oh, how I nearly forgot!" Kitty shook her head. "So much commotion has rendered my memory feeble. We have guests in our midst. Mr Bingley has arrived, accompanied by Mr and Mrs Hurst and Miss Bingley. Jane entreats you to rescue her as Mr Collins has succumbed to hysterics in the north parlour. Mary and Mama dare not abandon him for fear of his precipitating some outlandish action, and Jane cannot singlehandedly attend to all the visitors."

Lizzy swallowed hard. She dared not utter a word, let alone inquire as to the cause of Mr Collins' hysteria—a malady more frequently afflicting overly indulged ladies. Presumably, he had discovered the reason behind Lady Catherine's presence in Hertfordshire.

She allowed Kitty to guide her to the south parlour, where Jane greeted her with a grateful smile.

Elizabeth composed herself and feigned indifference towards the aged diary clasped in her hand.

Mr Hurst appeared half-slumbering, exhibiting little enthusiasm for the visit, while his wife perched upon a chair as though fearing it might transmit some dreadful ailment.

After Lizzy offered apologies for her unavailability upon the unexpected arrival of their guests, Miss Bingley remarked, "Oh, it matters not, Miss Eliza. Just imagine, you and dear Jane being connected to Mr Darcy! What an astonishing revelation it must have been."

Mr Bingley seemed ill at ease with his sister's effusive remarks, though he refrained from silencing her.

Elizabeth risked a glance at Jane and was unsurprised to find her sister's head bowed, and her cheeks tinged with a blush. It fell upon Lizzy to counter Miss Bingley's endeavour to form an attachment—a no doubt formidable obstacle in the lady's pursuit of Mr Darcy.

"Pray, Miss Bingley, whatever you may have heard shall make little difference to my sisters and me. We may indeed be related to Mr Darcy, but we are exceedingly modest and insignificant relations."

\*∧\*∧\*

Darcy was contemplating ways to get away from his relatives. He was starting to regret asking about Miss Bennets once he found out that Aunt Catherine would be giving her opinion on them. After being stuck between her and his uncle for several days, Darcy was sorry that he even had brought up the topic. Even drinking brandy helped not with the headaches he was experiencing.

In the midst of Colonel Fitzwilliam's tribulations with the militia and the shocking revelation of another horrible incident —a transgression so heinous that even Wickham, vile as he was, seemed incapable of stooping so low—Darcy could not help but covet his cousin's dearth of troublesome relations.

His own kin, it appeared, were determined to make his life an arduous trial, whether by intention or mere happenstance. Even Bingley and his sisters, along with the insufferable Hurst, had braved the inclement weather to pay a visit to Bennets. Undoubtedly, the tranquillity of Longbourn exceeded that of Netherfield.

If that was not vexing enough, the Earl's solicitor was due to arrive in a mere two days, intent on ascertaining the precise legal standing of Miss Bennets, a development that would undoubtedly provoke further contention. At least this legal arbiter would remain impervious to Aunt Catherine's artful persuasions; after all, she was not amongst his esteemed clients, nor was she ever likely to be.

Upon witnessing Mr Darcy's almost desperate plea for access to his esteemed library, Mr Bennet could have exhibited a modicum of surprise. However, it would have required a truly remarkable event to elicit such a reaction. To his credit, Bennet concealed his astonishment with admirable composure, granting the request without further comment.

The young man expressed his gratitude to the older one and sighed audibly. "Undoubtedly, this has been a tremendous shock for you as well, sir."

Mr Bennet's countenance betrayed an air of fatigue and ageing. "Indeed, it has been quite unsettling." A hint of amusement danced across his visage. "However, I declare your predicament has proven far more onerous than mine."

"One might agree," conceded Darcy, his concurrence slightly surprising even to himself. Not that Mr Bennet's observation lacked accuracy, but it was hardly a sentiment one readily admitted. "Our discussions have been rather spirited, to say the least."

"In that regard, I have no doubts," Bennet concurred, pouring a glass of brandy and extending it to his companion. "You are most welcome to seek solace within these walls. I hope you shall find a few items of interest here."

A wave of relief washed over Darcy upon realising that Mr Bennet had tactfully refrained from mentioning the other underlying motive for his visit to Longbourn and its well-stocked library. It would not do to disclose that he sought refuge from his relentless relatives.

Thankfully, Mr Bennet did possess a well-appointed collection of books. Darcy's claim of seeking congenial reading material was an entirely accurate one. Furthermore, the shelves were arranged in a manner that allowed for secluded nooks, concealed and tranquil corners furnished with weathered yet comfortable chairs, where one could read undisturbed, shielded from unwanted interruptions.

He selected a recent edition of Lord Byron's scandalous works and settled into one such cosy enclave, observing a faint waft of lavender tinged with a more familiar fragrance. Presumably, some of Miss Bennets also frequented these reading corners.

His surmise was swiftly validated as Miss Elizabeth entered the room, clutching an old and dust-covered book in one delicate hand.

Darcy involuntarily tensed, uncertain of the quick-witted young lady's opinion of him and his family.

To his surprise, the young woman merely arched a delicate eyebrow in his direction before gracefully taking the adjacent chair in the secluded corner. She tucked her legs beneath her in a most unladylike, yet entirely natural, manner and opened her book, her brow furrowing slightly as she read, her teeth gently biting her lower lip.

Darcy struggled to maintain focus on his own volume and found himself unable to divert his attention. Miss Elizabeth seemed entirely unaware of the myriad emotions that played across her countenance. Though he knew it was improper to peek at her so intimately, he could not tear his gaze away.

She should have been raised amongst his own family, he thought. With proper connections and the experiences of a London season, she would have been the belle of the ton. While her figure might not possess conventional perfection, her effortless grace and vivacious eyes conspired to create an impression of beauty that transcended mere physical attributes.

She was a woman who would never accept a marriage purely for the sake of social advantage. Darcy could not imagine her consenting to a proposal from a man she did not, at the very least, respect.

He sighed inwardly. If only Georgiana possessed the same

strength of character. Ever since the disastrous events in Ramsgate, she had seemed lost and broken, as if Wickham's heartless actions had crushed her spirit.

Eventually, Elizabeth looked up from her book and regarded him with unabashed curiosity. "Pray, Mr Darcy, do I sport a bird's nest atop my head or some other disfigurement? I dare say you have not read a single page since my arrival."

His cheeks warmed, unable to deny the truth of her observation regarding his lack of progress in reading. "I apologise, Miss Bennet. Your presence is, as always, captivating, and I found myself entranced by the depth of expression with which you immerse yourself in your reading."

A faint blush graced her cheeks, mirroring the warmth spreading across his own face. "Oh, dear. My mother often admonishes me for such a display, but I have never possessed the ability to resist becoming completely absorbed."

Darcy's lips twitched with amusement. "Alas, we cannot all meet Mrs Bennet's lofty standards."

"Indeed," she replied with a soft chuckle, "and I have often found myself lacking in that regard."

# Chapter 9

It was perhaps fortunate that the much-anticipated Netherfield ball should occur while that estate was occupied by its surfeit of notable guests: the presence of those guests ensured that the good people of Meryton were considerably more exercised in displaying their virtues both real and imagined to the visitors than in speculating about the purpose of such a gathering.

Elizabeth certainly welcomed the distraction the ball provided. She had, in the end, given her birth mother's diary to Mr Darcy after one of his visits—and after defeating him soundly in a game of chess, much to her father's amusement—and wished to hear nothing more of the matter.

That Jane was bereft of good sense in Mr Bingley's presence helped not one whit in Lizzy's opinion, while Mary had entirely lost her head to whatever charms the unfortunate Mr Collins presented. All of her sisters had nursed orphaned kittens and puppies to health, though none so fiercely as Mary. Lizzy could only think that Mary saw their cousin in the same light.

With Kitty and Lydia, both besotted by the romance of Jannie Bennet's life—it seemed not at all romantic to Elizabeth to risk everything for an uncertain future without even the surety of a suitor to save her from her folly—and Mr Bennet hiding in his study, Longbourn seemed far more confining than usual.

If that were not problem enough, it appeared that Colonel Forster had ceased to care about keeping his men under guard until the perpetrator of the attacks was found, for Denny, Wickham, and two others whose names Lizzy could not recall always seemed to be about in town whenever Elizabeth was there. Worse, it seemed to her that whenever her mother was distracted, Wickham would pay entirely too much attention to Catherine.

With the other young officers vying for Kitty's attention, no others noticed anything unusual. Wickham was always properly deferential when any attention was turned his way – so much so that Catherine could not be certain she truly saw improper attentions.

Or perhaps she was being too quick to judge? Still, Elizabeth found herself seeking to assure herself Wickham was nowhere near her sister as the night progressed.

Darcy, too, found the ball trying. His ears still rang from Aunt Catherine's accusation that he attended to spite his cousin Anne, who was, of course, too ill to attend.

Fitzwilliam had forewarned him that Forster had granted parole to all his officers, asserting the impracticability of keeping them within the encampment while the inquiries yielded no progress.

Darcy's self-control proved fortuitous, as Wickham, at least possessing the sensibility to maintain a considerable distance from Darcy, abided by the flow of the crowd.

His anticipation had been set upon relishing Miss Elizabeth's wit, yet it was lamentably absent. As the dance concluded, she expressed her regret for her preoccupation and hoped that she had not entirely marred the evening for him.

"Miss Elizabeth, you possess the remarkable ability to enhance evenings rather than mar them." Though slightly startled by his own audacious flattery, Darcy could not lament his words, particularly when the young lady blushed and responded with a charming smile.

"Truly, sir, you have spent an excess of time in the company of your cousin, Colonel Fitzwilliam, for I would swear it was he who bestowed such audacious compliments."

He smiled, unable to conceal his amusement. "There was a period, Miss Elizabeth, when the two of us were deemed the greatest scoundrels in the county."

She arched an eyebrow. "Indeed? It seems quite incongruous. I am convinced you were a solemn and studious child who never gave your parents even the slightest cause for concern."

Darcy chuckled. "If my parents were present to inquire, they would assure you that you are gravely mistaken, madam. No doubt they would regale you with tales of my youthful indiscretions simply to establish the point."

"Impossible!" declared she. "You could not have committed any childhood indiscretions. Now, I, on the other hand, have been an incorrigible hoyden, guilty of countless transgressions, from scaling trees that far exceeded a child's capacity to the inexplicable appearance of frogs in my mother's bed."

Darcy felt his lips twitching. "I recollect receiving a well-deserved thrashing for a comparable offence," confessed he. "Father was resolute in his belief that I should remember that young gentlemen ought not to populate a lady's bed with amphibious creatures."

He was rewarded with one of Elizabeth's radiant smiles. "If young gentlemen refrain from such actions, then assuredly you did not partake."

Unfortunately, the interlude was all too brief, for the lady was soon claimed for another dance, leaving Darcy to ponder her steadfast regard. However, her liveliness was transient, as that haunted and somewhat distant expression returned to her countenance after Bingley led her back to the dance floor.

He retreated to the shadows, quietly amused by the throng surrounding his cousins. A Viscount and a Colonel would invariably overshadow a mere Mister in terms of associations, a fact that Darcy did not regret. Conviviality was not his inclination; he far preferred the tranquillity of his library or the serenity of Pemberley's grounds.

His thoughts drifted to the aged diary Elizabeth had presented to him. Through its pages, the late Mrs Bennet unveiled herself as a heedless and impulsive girl who had never truly experienced a mother's undying love. Darcy could comprehend why she had ultimately decided to run away from Rosings. Alongside Lady Catherine's temper, there had been the notion of not being Sir Lewis's daughter, the deception that had been too much to bear for sixteen years old girl.

In truth, Darcy suspected that the most arduous battle would be to extricate Aunt Catherine from the comforts of Rosings Park and relocate her to the London townhouse her late husband had provided. It was unquestionable that his aunt would not content herself with the income provided; she was far too accustomed to being the mistress of Rosings, with all the privileges it entailed.

Alas, secrets of such magnitude could not be concealed for long. The connection between the Bennets and Fitzwilliams, initiated by a tumultuous argument at Netherfield Park, had begun to leak within hours. Though the servants of Longbourn were too loyal and respectful to engage in gossip, the same could not be said for those in the employ of Netherfield.

Given the esteemed status of the Bennet family in the district and their popularity, many who spread the tidings revelled in the notion that Miss Bennets would now have the opportunity to marry into more elevated circles rather than being confined to the limited society of Meryton.

The observer at the ball found this information worth pondering. Soon, he would have to depart the area, as his necessary activities precluded him from remaining in one place for an extended period. Even in the most wretched corners of London, he could not guarantee to satisfy his insatiable cravings for more than a few months without causing a scandalous uproar. He abhorred this loathsome compulsion, yet he had never been able to suppress it. The smallest provocation, be it anger or frustration, could ignite it. If he could find no alternative but to target those least likely to be missed, this vile impulse would drive him towards the hangman's noose.

His gaze briefly fixed upon the cause of his affliction, the man who had thwarted his plans at every turn while remaining blissfully unaware of the depths to which he had driven him. Dwelling on what might have served little purpose. His adversary had firmly established himself here, his fortune continuously favouring him while simultaneously mocking his antagonist. Weariness enveloped him, for it seemed that wherever he went, his enemy followed, driving him unwittingly.

Preparations for his departure had been made, and the debts he had incurred would occupy his adversary's attention for a considerable time. All he required was the consent of the chosen mark, who would provide a plausible motive for his flight, wholly divergent from his true purpose. Her attractiveness and innocence offered some solace; perhaps she possessed enough charm to assuage the demons within him momentarily.

If not... well, he would confront that when the time came.

*∧*∧*

To declare that the ultimate settlement of Sir Lewis's testament was not met with universal approbation would be tantamount to asserting that relations between England and France bore a slight hint of unease. Darcy ardently yearned for a scheme to placate Aunt Catherine through the rational application of brandy in order to allay her agitations.

When she endeavoured to strike the hapless lawyers with her cane—an implement she had no need of for perambulation but which furnished her a formidable weapon should anyone arouse her ire—Darcy responded impulsively, hastening to relieve his aunt of the cane's grip.

"Pray, be seated, Aunt. You are exhibiting a spectacle of foolishness." Darcy pondered upon the genesis of his newfound candour. It seemed he had omitted to fortify himself with brandy, therefore absolving it from the role of causation.

"I shall not endure this... travesty!" Lady Catherine remained impervious to persuasion. "My dear departed husband would never have countenanced such an affront."

Darcy pressed her—gently, albeit resolutely—back into her seat. "Pray, Aunt, are you endowed with the faculty of reading?"

The veiled affront rendered Lady Catherine momentarily speechless, though alas, not for an extended duration. "You ungrateful—"

Darcy cast a stern gaze across the room. His uncle and cousins ought to have lent their aid instead of endeavouring to suppress their mirth. "Randall, if you would be so kind as to retain the will? I shall hold Aunt Catherine's hands." It would not bode well if she were to rend the will asunder in a fit of rage.

Darcy sidestepped and clasped her hands while his aunt sputtered in incoherent fury. "You are overly agitated, Aunt. Now, if you would be gracious enough to peruse the document Randall is preserving, we may lay to rest any doubts that persist in your mind. Is that not the handwriting of Sir Lewis?"

Following yet another diatribe, this time against the callousness of her nephews and their proscription from ever setting foot in her home, Lady Catherine ultimately acquiesced, conceding that the script was indeed that of Sir Lewis.

Darcy employed a gentle tone as he spoke, "I am beholden to you, Aunt. I implore you to read the document on our behalf."

She endeavoured to extricate her hands, but though Darcy maintained a gentle hold, he refused to grant her release. Eventually, after casting withering glances throughout the room and affronting each individual present, she commenced her reading.

Darcy was quite certain that the will contained no

aspersions upon his father's or Lady Fitzwilliam's lineage, nor did it comprise the numerous references to ungrateful relatives that seasoned Lady Catherine's perusal. Nevertheless, the essence of the testament remained unequivocally apparent: Sir Lewis had urged his executor from undertaking any duties save those compelled by necessity until the fate of his missing daughter, Janet, was ascertained. If Janet de Bourgh were indeed living, she would inherit. Should she meet her demise without offspring, Anne stood as the heiress.

Sir Lewis had even made provisions in the event of his daughters' putative children: Janet's son, if she were to bear one, followed by the eldest daughter, and so forth. With four Bennet daughters, the probability of Anne de Bourgh inheriting Rosings Park seemed tenuous at best.

There existed no doubt that Miss Bennets were the progeny of Janet de Bourgh—the diary discovered by Elizabeth Bennet had provided conclusive evidence. And though it also revealed that Janet had believed she was not de Bourgh by blood, Sir Lewis had not been aware of that fact. He had recognised Janet as his offspring and his heir. The latest development could not have had any impact on his will.

Therefore, Miss Bennet stood as the rightful inheritor of Rosings Park, while the other Miss Bennets were entitled to a substantial dowry. As for Anne, she was bequeathed one of the de Bourgh townhouses along with a handsome sum of fifty thousand pounds, though Sir Lewis had expressed his desire for his daughters to dwell together at Rosings.

Darcy harboured doubts as to whether any of Miss Bennets would appreciate their newfound fortunes, for the stipulations outlined in Sir Lewis's will superseded the far simpler testament left behind by their birth mother.

That Lady Catherine would denounce Miss Bennets as the most abominable breed of fortune-seekers was an inevitability. Unconfined by any semblance of restraint, her ladyship had come to believe that a mere declaration on her part sufficed to bend reality to her whims.

Darcy fervently hoped to avoid the arduous task of relocating his aunt from Rosings Park to the townhouse bequeathed to her by her late husband. Such an endeavour would test the most generous of dispositions—a quality not even his closest confidants would assert he possessed.

*∧*∧*

Upon the arrival of Darcy, the Earl, and his son at Longbourn, Elizabeth's keen intuition led her to suspect the nature of their visit. Her suspicions were confirmed when Jane was summoned to Mr Bennet's library while the gentlemen comfortably ensconced themselves within its walls.

Lizzy's apprehension heightened as Jane emerged from the library, her countenance resembling the time she had discovered a frog nestled in her bed. In spite of knowing full well that, on this occasion, the frog was strictly metaphorical and not of Jane's own making, Elizabeth found little solace in such knowledge.

Contrary to Lizzy's childhood perception, Jane's virtuous nature was not feigned or contrived to garner admiration within their lively and exuberant family. Elizabeth had come to realise that her sister was as tender and forgiving as her outward demeanour suggested. The only aspect Jane concealed were her most intense emotions, adeptly masked beneath her customary comportment.

Elizabeth grasped her sister's hands. "Jane! Your hands are chilled to the bone. Come, sit down and partake of some tea." Though consumed by curiosity, Lizzy refrained from inquiring about the contents of Jane's conversation that had occurred in the library. She knew better than to press her sister for information; Jane would reveal it in due course.

Fortuitously, they found respite in the seclusion of the south parlour as the three younger girls had departed for Meryton, accompanied by their mother and Mr Collins.

Jane's hands trembled, though she managed to prevent any spillage of tea. After two cups, both sweetened with a lavish amount of honey surpassing her usual preference, Jane placed the cup delicately on the saucer and sighed. "Oh, Lizzy, it is utterly dreadful!" She shook her head. "The Earl has declared me the heiress of Sir Lewis de Bourgh, and there exists no remedy to alter this circumstance in spite of the fact that Janet de Bourgh was not his flesh and blood."

Knowing full well what was to come, Lizzy remained silent.

"Poor Miss de Bourgh!" Jane intertwined her hands in distress. "I would never desire to supplant her, but it appears I have no choice."

"Surely Miss de Bourgh has not been entirely disregarded?" Elizabeth's opinion of Sir Lewis would be far from flattering if he had overlooked his younger daughter in favour of the elder.

"No... However, her expectations have been significantly diminished."

Lizzy recognised the shock that must have accompanied such a revelation. She herself had yet to fully accept the fact that her birth mother had been Lady Catherine's sister but raised as her daughter—a notion she still found difficult to fathom. "And what of Lady Catherine?" Lizzy pondered aloud. That formidable lady could not have taken this news lightly. "She must be greatly perturbed."

Jane frowned. "The Earl informed me that Lady Catherine had adamantly refused to acknowledge us. However, Mr Darcy asserted that she was amply provided for and," Jane hesitated, her expression pained, "deserved a taste of humility."

Elizabeth arched an eyebrow in surprise. Such a remark might be expected from Colonel Fitzwilliam, but Mr Darcy, who was notably ill at ease in social gatherings, retreating into a shell of formality? It would have seemed inconceivable if not for the fact that Lizzy also considered it implausible that she and her sisters were related to individuals as well-connected as the Earl and his esteemed family.

The Bennet family, though possessing an ancient lineage and firmly established in society, had never been counted among the innermost circles of the ton. The Gardiners, on the other hand, were regarded by societal standards as occupying a position far beneath even that. It was one of the reasons why Elizabeth viewed society merely as an arbitrary nuisance. She found as much merit in Uncle Gardiner's thriving business and burgeoning wealth as in the more refined pursuits of gentlemen.

Indeed, Mr Gardiner's circumstances surpassed those of many a gentleman who scoffed at his acquired fortune. He faced no difficulties when it came to providing for his children.

Elizabeth's ears were promptly alerted to the impending arrival of the visitors by the sound of approaching footsteps. Jane's countenance now bore a livelier hue, and her hands no longer quivered in trepidation.

In the company of the three gentlemen, Mr Bennet entered the parlour and inquired, "My dears, pray tell, where might your sisters be?"

Lizzy and Jane gracefully rose to welcome their guests while Mrs Hill hurriedly attended to their tea and procured additional china.

Elizabeth dutifully informed her father that they had ventured to Meryton.

"Did our cousin accompany them?"

"Yes, Papa," Jane responded, her customary serenity untarnished.

Tea was served, and it was then that Mr Bennet, his customary mirth undeterred by the weighty news that had just been conveyed to him, uttered, "Well, my dears, it appears that I have the woeful duty of informing you that our tranquil Hertfordshire corner shall soon be besieged by fortune-seeking young gentlemen, all of whom I shall endeavour to repel with whatever skills I still possess."

The Earl's eyes twinkled, although his countenance remained unchanged. "Oh, really, sir, you do exaggerate. You shall have my aid in shielding off the undeserving suitors, and I dare say my sons and nephew shall contribute theirs as well."

Elizabeth supposed it was fortunate that his lordship had developed an affinity for her father, though she remained far from sanguine regarding the changes in her circumstances.

"That, your ladyship, is a privilege reserved for a father," Mr Bennet replied with a smile. He nodded in Lizzy's direction. "Jane has already been apprised of her favourable circumstances. Elizabeth, I must inform you that you and your sisters possess a dowry of twenty thousand pounds."

Lizzy swallowed, her mouth abruptly parched. Such a sum! "How... How is this possible?" she finally managed to inquire. "And what of Lady Catherine and Miss de Bourgh?"

The Earl emitted a soft chuckle. "Sir Lewis was immensely wealthy; he made his fortune in India, my dear niece. Much of his has been held in trust since his demise, and his investments have continued to yield lucrative returns. My sister shall inherit de Bourgh House in London and an ample income to meet her needs. Anne shall acquire one of the townhouses Sir Lewis possessed in addition to her fifty thousand pounds." His expression softened. "You need not fret over Anne's welfare; she shall be well provided for."

"Thank you, sir," Jane murmured softly. "I... I hope she chooses to remain—Rosings is her home."

"Simply keep her apart from Aunt Catherine, and all shall be well," Lord Fitzwilliam interjected in a low voice.

His father rolled his eyes and shook his head. "I hold no apprehensions regarding Anne's adjustment." He sighed. "I do beseech you to grant your aunt more time: my sister is not taking this development kindly."

The Viscount leaned forward. "Father's statement, as always, falls short of the mark. Lady Catherine indulges in one of her notorious tantrums and insists that she shall never vacate Rosings, nor shall she acknowledge anyone except Anne as the rightful heir of Rosings." He paused and contemplated. "Perhaps she needs to spend more time in Mrs Bennet's company. I am certain Aunt Catherine would greatly benefit from a friend of her sensible disposition."

Elizabeth observed a barely perceptible twitch of Mr Darcy's lips, indicating that he, too, found amusement in the prospect of Mrs Bennet's straightforward practicality being brought to bear on his aunt. And truth be told, Lizzy could hardly fault him for it.

"In any case, my dears," Mr Bennet resumed after a brief pause, "You need no longer harbour concerns for your future in the unfortunate event of my departure from this world before you secure suitable matches. I do not doubt that Rosings Park is more than spacious enough to accommodate all of you, and Jane shall find it nearly impossible to deny you all." He shook his head, a wry smile forming. "I do hope the estate possesses a competent steward."

"He would indeed prove excellent, were it not for Lady Catherine's perpetual inclination to override him," remarked Darcy. "Surely you have observed her rather... entrenched habits."

As polite understatements went, Darcy's comment was truly remarkable.

# Chapter 10

Bennets held a place of great esteem in Meryton society; therefore, news of their newfound prosperity and elevated connections spread like wildfire, encompassing the entire town within the span of a day. While there existed a certain degree of bewilderment over Jannie Gardiner's true identity as Janet de Bourgh, so it was whispered. Consequently, Mrs Phillips received accolades for her benevolence towards her adopted sister.

As the removal of Miss Bennets elevated them to a loftier social sphere, Mrs Phillips bore no ill will, for her own daughters now stood amongst the most eligible young ladies in the district. The revelation of a deception spanning over two decades was rendered inconsequential.

To Miss Bennets, the reception they received from the locals displayed little change, though the noticeable increase in attention from the officers did not escape their notice. It seemed only natural that an attractive young lady with a substantial dowry would garner more interest from an officer subsisting on a limited salary than an equally appealing damsel of modest means. Yet, this state of affairs, far from commendable, failed to inspire admiration.

Jane's heart was already claimed by Mr Bingley, causing her to be oblivious to the heightened deference around her. Meanwhile, Mary diligently worked her charms on Mr Collins, transforming him into a genial young man who greatly benefited from the company of a lady whose education and inclinations harmonised so well with his own.

Lydia, unaffected by the officers' attentions, appeared to regard them as nothing more than her due, showing no partiality towards any particular man, mostly because she was still not out and her mother kept a close eye on her. Elizabeth suspected that her sister merely relished in the novelty of it all, as any young lady recently embarking upon the marriage market might be inclined to do.

Catherine, however, proved an exception. She revelled in the romance of the situation and chafed under the vigilant watch of Mrs Bennet. Lizzy feared for her sister's vulnerability, concerned that the impressionable Kitty might succumb to the seductive allurements Wickham showered upon her whenever Mrs Bennet's attention wavered.

Aware of the limitations of a single individual, Elizabeth knew well that her mother could not be omnipresent or witness all occurrences. Regrettably, the improper advances of a handsome young officer posed a far greater threat than frogs inhabiting Jane's bedchamber. The latter might evoke surprise or distress, yet it would not tarnish their reputations.

Finding an opportune moment to alert Mrs Bennet offered a more formidable challenge than initially presumed. The newfound family of Miss Bennets sought their company on a near-daily basis, or so it seemed. However, Elizabeth found solace in the fact that Lady Catherine refrained from gracing these events with her presence. Indeed, that estimable lady did not venture to Longbourn, and whenever Bennets visited Netherfield, she conveniently suffered from minor ailments too trivial to warrant genuine concern but significant enough to exempt her from joining her relatives.

During those visits, Mr Bingley proved a most exemplary host, fulfilling all expectations, while his sister assumed the role of an attentive yet insincere hostess. As for the Hursts, Elizabeth's encounters with them remained infrequent, though she detected a covert amusement lurking within their countenances whenever they observed Miss Bingley.

Meanwhile, the Earl's assertion that Mr Bingley was an unsuitable match for his niece due to his wealth being amassed in trade sparked a spirited debate. However, the couple seemed blissfully unaware of the contentious matter.

In response to the insinuation that a mere parson— whose patron happened to be her aunt—was beneath her, Mary displayed a tremendous fervour in defence of Mr Collins, supporting her utterance by quoting Fordyce and Shakespeare.

Lord Fitzwilliam's evident delight and amusement at the entire affair did little to assuage Elizabeth's composure. It appeared that he and Mr Darcy were engaged in a less-than-subtle competition for her affections, though the Viscount's attentions resembled those of an elder brother more than Mr Darcy's.

Therefore, it came as no surprise that Catherine's sudden disappearance, occurring less than a week after the revelation of the improved fortunes of Miss Bennets, struck with the resounding force of a thunderclap.

Mrs Bennet and Lizzy were preparing to inspect the estate and its tenants when a pale-faced housekeeper summoned them to the still room—the most secluded part of the house.

"Hill? Has something happened?" asked Camila.

The folded paper proffered by Hill's outstretched hand was sufficient to quell Mrs Bennet's inquiries, particularly when she recognised Kitty's unmistakable handwriting. Her hands trembled as she unfolded the paper and gave it to Lizzy, unveiling the words inscribed within.

Elizabeth read it aloud:

> My dearest family, I beseech you not to judge me too harshly, for I am undeniably in love. My beloved Lieutenant Wickham and I are eloping to Gretna Green,

for we wish to be married, and George is certain that the
Earl will never permit such a union between his niece and
a mere officer.

With love and regret,

Catherine Bennet (soon to bear the name Wickham)

The paper slipped from Lizzy's nerveless fingers and
gracefully descended to the floor.

"Mama, what shall we do?" uttered she.

Mrs Bennet swallowed hard, struggling to suppress the
overwhelming urge to weep.

"Poor, misguided Kitty!" Lizzy continued in anguish. "To have
been deceived by a man who undoubtedly had his sights set on
her share of the de Bourgh fortune.

"Hill," spoke Mrs Bennet when she recovered her senses,
"Please summon Mr Bennet and my daughters to the northern
parlour," she managed to utter, her voice choked with emotion.
"And ensure that those in attendance are made aware of the
utmost confidentiality regarding this matter."

The housekeeper nodded solemnly, executing a curtsey. "I
shall instruct Hannah to prepare some tea."

A sombre assembly awaited them: Jane weeping silently,
Lydia pale and nervously wringing her handkerchief, Mary
seated motionless. And as for Mr Bennet, his countenance bore a
hue of grey rather than the usual pallor, and his trembling hands
struggled to retain the tea within his cup.

Though Lizzy ardently desired nothing more than to escape
the entire abominable situation, she found herself unable to do
so. Amidst the calamity of Catherine's elopement, she appeared
to be the sole individual capable of rising above the horrors that
had befallen them.

"Kitty believes that Mr Wickham will escort her to Gretna

Green," her voice quivered, frail and feeble. "However, we cannot ascertain the veracity of her claims." She swallowed and blinked persistently until her vision cleared.

"Mr Bennet, we ought to dispatch trustworthy individuals to scour the roads," his wife addressed him, trying to sound stronger than she felt. "Surely they cannot pass unnoticed."

"My dear, we are clueless as to their mode of travel," he replayed and closed his weary eyes. "They may very well be on horseback themselves."

"Three hundred miles on horseback?" Mary whispered in wonder.

Even after Elizabeth took a deep breath, the tightness in her chest refused to relent. "Kitty took a valise and her lace basket. Such articles cannot be carried on horseback."

Mrs Bennet nodded. "No, they must have some vehicle. Perhaps they travel by post."

"Would you be so kind as to make the arrangements, Mrs Bennet?" her husband pleaded, his voice breathless. "I find myself—"

"Papa!"

Of all those present, it was Camila who reached Mr Bennet first, steadying her husband as he teetered in his seat and swiftly undoing his coat.

From Elizabeth's perspective, it felt like she watched the scene unfold from a distance. She rose to her feet and called for assistance in carrying her father to his chamber, as well as for someone to fetch the doctor. It was that composed version of Lizzy who dispatched Mary to the still room for the soothing lavender tincture that alleviated tension and Lydia to concoct a fresh batch of herbal rub to relieve strain on the heart and lungs.

Meanwhile, Mrs Bennet tended to her husband, a profound worry and anguish etched on her countenance.

Elizabeth often wondered at the nature of her parents'

relationship. Of course, they had Lydia together, but it seemed like they were more apart than together these last many years. And while she could not fathom her father's feelings, she now could see how much Camila Bennet carried for him. Had her father ever recognised how heavily he relied upon his wife and that she deserved more than a mere acknowledgement?

How often Elizabeth reminded the servants and her sisters that the absence of Kitty must not be spoken of, she could not precisely tell. The disgraceful truth could not remain concealed for an extended period, but for now, it must be confined within the confines of their home.

They let the inhabitants of Meryton believe that Longbourn shunned visitors due to Mr Bennet's indisposition. In due course, it was an accurate account.

Scarcely had the doctor ascended the stairs when the housekeeper informed Lizzy that Mr Bingley and Mr Darcy waited in the foyer.

The composed and collected Elizabeth requested that Hill guide them to the parlour and arrange for tea to be served. She would apologise for the household's disarray and seek their... Lizzy was not entirely certain what she should beseech of the gentlemen, only that she held trust in both of them.

Curiously, it was Mr Darcy who blurted out, "Good God! What has happened?"

Elizabeth would have anticipated such an impulsive reaction from Mr Bingley, not his restrained companion.

"Our father has fallen ill. The doctor is currently attending to him: we implore your forgiveness for our lack of hospitality."

"But of course!" Bingley hastened to Jane's side, clasping her hands in his own. "How may we be of assistance?"

Elizabeth swallowed hard. The façade of composure was crumbling.

"I am not sure, sir. I think it might be my father's heart. He has had too many shocks," she said, her voice choked with emotion. She tried to hold back tears, not wanting to cry in front of her sisters or Mr Darcy, who was now holding her hands for comfort. However, she could not stop the tears from flowing, and she felt overwhelmed when Hill entered the room to inform them that the vicar was needed.

The world seemed to fade away.

*∧*∧*

Kitty found herself nestled in the secluded corner of the carriage, striving to maintain an air of composure and tranquillity. The current circumstances weighed heavily upon her, for everything had taken an unexpected turn, leaving her disconcerted and disheartened.

Initially, she had been captivated by Mr Wickham's grand gesture of whisking her away in such a splendid carriage. His demeanour had exuded an air of refined courtesy at first, but as the carriage veered onto the London road instead of the anticipated northward path, his temper grew irritable. He sharply reprimanded her for suppressing her trivial prattle.

While she hesitated to voice her concerns, a sense of trepidation engulfed her when Mr Wickham commenced imbibing directly from a jug containing a liquid that emitted a repugnant odour reminiscent of the wretched libations served in Meryton's most disreputable taverns. Kitty had never partaken in such a diabolical brew herself, but her familiarity was limited to the olfactory impressions left by patrons frequenting those unsavoury establishments and her mother's acerbic commentary on the calibre of individuals who would dare to indulge in such a state publicly.

To the girl's admittedly circumscribed knowledge in such matters, Mr Wickham seemed well on his way to succumbing to a similar level of intoxication.

The carriage swayed and jostled recklessly, propelled by

an excessive velocity that threatened to unsettle them all. Clutching her delicate lace basket, Catherine silently implored the heavens that the unfortunate horse would not falter, for at such breakneck speed, catastrophe surely loomed.

As Wickham finally set the jug aside, the dim illumination, barely permeating through the drawn shades, obscured Kitty's ability to discern whether his countenance bore a smile, a sneer, or something far more sinister.

"Well, my dear, this is far from the idyllic scenario you had envisioned, is it not?"

Summoning every ounce of courage within her, Catherine mustered a response. "Indeed, dear Mr Wickham, one's literary indulgences display such exploits involving ladders rather than grand carriages."

His laughter rang out. "Even someone of my ilk can procure assistance in fulfilling the yearnings of my heart."

This revelation hinted that the carriage had been borrowed, prompting Catherine to ponder the identity of the lender and their ulterior motives. Surely, no affluent benefactor would lend such a vehicle to an officer with scant prospects merely for the purpose of elopement. Striving to feign awe and admiration, she uttered, "Your resourcefulness knows no bounds, dear sir."

Wickham emitted yet another of those unsightly chuckles. "A man in my predicament possesses few alternatives, my dear."

"Undoubtedly, your cunning and ingenuity will undoubtedly aid your ascension through the ranks of society."

The sound emanating from Wickham's lips bore an inscrutable meaning, save for the unmistakable absence of praise, not even for himself.

He drew nearer, and the man's proximity caused Kitty to suppress the urge to wrinkle her nose or display any sign of distaste. Where had the charming young officer disappeared to? More importantly, what lay beneath the façade he so skillfully projected?

"And so, my dear, how shall we occupy ourselves until we reach our destination?" His breath exuded a noxious stench.

Catherine put on a smile and suggested to the man, "Perhaps it is time for some rest, sir. After all, we still have a long journey ahead to reach Gretna Green."

"Is that all?" the man asked, making the girl feel uneasy.

Realising the man's intentions, she reasoned with him, "We are not married yet, sir. Do not you think it is better to wait a little longer?"

Wickham let out a loud, drunken laugh and blew warm breath, tainted with alcohol, in her face. "You are so modest, my dear. A day or two early shall not hurt."

Catherine knew that no honourable man would ever suggest such a thing, so she froze, unable to respond.

Wickham swiftly seized her delicate lace basket, relieving her of its burden, and placed it alongside her valise. Before Kitty could conjure a coherent response, he loomed over her, straddling her legs, and leaned down to initiate a kiss.

If it could be labelled as such, for it lacked the tenderness that Kitty had gleaned from the clandestine perusal of novels skillfully hidden from her mother's watchful eye. Instead, Wickham's intoxicating breath collided with her lips, forcibly pressed against hers. His intrusive tongue invaded the confines of her mouth while his ungentle hand ventured down towards her outer garment.

Summoning a surge of strength borne out of sheer terror, Catherine instinctively propelled both legs upwards. In her instinctive motion, her knee found the tender flesh—that vulnerable part of a man's anatomy.

A startled yelp escaped the man's lips as he stumbled, ungracefully landing on the opposite seat.

Noticing the effect of her action, Kitty kicked once more without hesitation, ensuring the pointed toe of her walking boot collided with his shin. She repeated this action when he stooped to attend to his injury, this time successfully striking his head.

He tumbled onto the carriage floor, defeated.

Suppressing a sob, Kitty swallowed her fear and trepidation.

"You shameless harlot!" Wickham's inebriation hindered any possibility of him regaining his footing from the rocking carriage floor.

Catherine delivered another resolute kick and then another until Wickham succumbed to the carriage floor, breathless and fatigued.

This time, she took no chances. In spite of the precarious footing and Wickham's occupation of most of the floor, Kitty mustered the courage to rise and launched a vigorous blow to his head, targeting the area just behind his ear. According to Papa's anatomical studies, this precise spot had the potential to render a man unconscious for an extended duration.

A slight twitch coursed through Wickham's body, and his breathing subsided into hushed stillness.

Catherine fervently hoped she had not inadvertently ended his life.

The mere thought of the girls who had perished sent shivers down her spine. Could Wickham be held accountable for their tragic fate? There was something amiss in his demeanour, something she had failed to notice earlier. His actions were not merely bereft of principles; they were deeply, abhorrently reprehensible.

She choked back a sob, refusing to succumb to despair. She must not remain in this carriage when it reached its final destination, but she possessed nothing save for her attire and her lace basket.

Kitty's trembling hands embarked on a search of Wickham's person, finding solace in the strong and steady rhythm of his heartbeat, confirming that she had not brought about his demise. Therefore, she needed not to confront the spectre of execution for the charge of murder.

Within Wickham's possession, she discovered a weighty pouch brimming with silver coins, an unreadable note in the dim twilight, and a flintlock pistol. Her decision to appropriate these belongings proved fortuitous. With the coins, she could secure lodging if need be and, perchance, even defend herself. Most importantly, by confiscating the weapon, she ensured that Wickham could not employ it against her.

The note might offer an explanation as to how he had come to acquire the carriage.

Carefully, Catherine stowed all these newfound possessions within her lace basket and drew it closer along with her valise, inching towards the adjacent carriage door. She steadied herself using the seat walls for support and cautiously swung open the door.

Moonlight flooded in, accompanied by a symphony of sounds. Kitty clutched the door frame with unwavering resolve, immersing herself in the scene unfolding before her. She could not risk leaping out where no soft landing awaited her descent.

A darkened line materialised, drawing nearer—a wall or, with any luck, a hedge. Catherine silently prayed for the latter, hoping the driver would not hear the carriage door colliding against its side. Gradually, the softened outlines confirmed the presence of a hedge.

Gathering her resolve before it had a chance to waver, Kitty clutched her valise tightly in one hand while the other gripped the precious lace basket. With a surge of determination, she propelled herself forward and took the leap.

The carriage sped onward, leaving Kitty ensconced within the hedge, her heart and body aching. For a prolonged interval, she remained motionless, the stifled sobs emanating from her being the only evidence of her continued existence.

Eventually, she summoned the strength to pull herself upright and stumbled onto the road, dragging her valise and lace basket in tow. She veered away from the path the carriage had taken, embarking on a weary trudge back towards Meryton.

Concealment became imperative—Catherine presented a dishevelled spectacle. If anyone could recognise her, the consequences could be severe indeed, but she knew she must return home and offer her sincerest apologies to Mama and Papa. She had inflicted disgrace upon herself and her loved ones, succumbing to foolish romantic notions.

Tears blurred her vision as she plodded onward. How had she allowed herself to be so gullible? She should have discerned that no honourable man would court a girl without her father's consent and whisk her away from her home under the pretence of love.

The least she could do was remain concealed until she reached the sanctuary of her home, where she could atone for her transgressions. And then... Kitty's thoughts faltered, unable to grapple with what lay ahead.

What had Mother said in times of adversity? One step at a time. Only one step could be taken at a time. Kitty had once dismissed it as a mere triviality, yet now, she comprehended the wisdom behind those words. To venture beyond her limits would surely lead to her downfall.

Her heart was heavy with remorse; she fervently wished to unburden herself of these thoughts.

# Chapter 11

Elizabeth found herself unable to measure the passing of time. The boundaries between day and night merged into a misty grey haze, where one indistinguishable moment seamlessly bled into another. Serene and resolute, she assumed the role of the composed Lizzy—the one who entrusted Hill with the task of convincing the household staff that Kitty's absence was due to her illness. It fell upon her to arrange for a trundle bed to be placed in her father's chamber for Mrs Bennet, who refused to abandon him even in her desperate need for rest. Elizabeth sat vigilantly, listening to the laborious struggle of her father's breath while her mother succumbed to sleep—a shared responsibility among Lizzy and her sisters.

The taste of food had become insipid, consumed solely out of obligation to the maintenance of Longbourn's affairs, whether its master was well or not. In the mundane tasks that occupied her mind, Elizabeth sought solace, temporarily shielding herself from the weight of other concerns.

Unexpectedly, Mr Collins became a source of comfort to them all, attending to any duty requiring a man's aid, his efforts never accompanied by a complaint. His tentative offer to assist in the management of Longbourn, coupled with his modest observation that he had no intention of laying claim to the estate while the master of the house was gravely ill, served to redeem him from the unfavourable impression he had initially made.

Elizabeth vaguely sensed a growing camaraderie between Mary and Mr Collins, a bond that appeared as though they were already wed, each deferring to the other when necessary. She also knew that news of Kitty's elopement would inevitably permeate through society, for her father's illness could not indefinitely shroud such information. Yet, all of these concerns felt inconsequential.

Sleep eluded her unless her body succumbed to utter exhaustion, its duration restricted to the bare minimum dictated by necessity. She could not ascertain the day, much less the hour, when she slipped out of the house through a side door, intent on harvesting from the herb garden.

The dim pre-dawn light surprised her but not nearly as much as the dishevelled figure awaiting her outside the door.

"Kitty?"

Elizabeth's eyes did not deceive her. Catherine let out a choked sob and flung herself into her sister's embrace.

"Hush," Lizzy whispered, cradling her sister, her fingers delicately caressing the rough, tangled locks. "You are home now, safe and sound."

Yet Kitty's distress only intensified. "Oh, Lizzy! I am so deeply sorry," she sobbed, her voice catching in her throat. "I had no inkling..." She shuddered. "Can you ever find it in your heart to forgive me?"

Though anger surged within her, Elizabeth suppressed it, recognising that Kitty could not comprehend the rash actions that had set everything in motion. She already bore enough remorse without the weight of their father's illness upon her soul.

"Of course," replied she with a calmness that belied her genuine emotions. "Now, come. We must get you indoors and to your bed. We have successfully maintained the facade of your illness; let it now become a reality."

Kitty blinked, but she did not resist her sister's gentle

command, nor did she question the employment of the rarely traversed back stairs. The servants would be partaking in their breakfast at this early hour, leaving the rest of the house shrouded in silence. Lizzy saw no reason to take unnecessary risks.

They arrived at Kitty's chamber unseen by prying eyes. Elizabeth closed the door softly, exhaling a long, weary sigh. Her sister stood by the narrow bed, clutching her basket as though her very life depended on it. In the dimness, her pallor was strikingly evident.

"Lizzy?"

"Come, change into your nightdress."

For a brief moment, attending to the matter of returning Kitty's garments to the wardrobe and aiding her in the process of changing provided enough distraction for Elizabeth to evade unwelcome thoughts. Presenting Catherine's time away as days spent in a sickbed could account for her dishevelled hair, while any dirt or grass stains on her dress could be attributed to the general tumult reigning over the household.

She fetched water from the jug—a stale supply, yet seemingly inconsequential—and settled down beside her sister. "Now, let me recount what transpired subsequent to your... departure."

Kitty winced, her expression filled with remorse.

Summoning her inner strength, Lizzy took a deep breath. "Papa fell ill," began she, omitting the triggering effect of the elopement note. "His heart... He has remained confined to his bed since the very day you left, and we all keep a constant vigil by his side."

Kitty clasped Lizzy's hand, her grip desperate. "I never... Oh, Lizzy! I am consumed by regret! Please tell me, will he recover?"

"We pray fervently for his health." There existed no other response Elizabeth could provide. "The most treacherous period was in the aftermath of the attack, yet he still languishes in a precarious state." She maintained her grasp on her sister's hand. "Kitty, only a select few are aware of your absence. Most believe that you succumbed to an illness brought on by Papa's assault."

The girl's fingers tightened around Lizzy's, her voice trembling. "Perhaps there is more truth to that than it initially appears," uttered she bitterly. "I acted the fool."

Elizabeth gently squeezed her sister's hand, striving to reassure her beleaguered sibling. "So, he deceived you," she uttered with an uncanny calmness, considering the tempestuous emotions that roiled within her. "I held apprehensions to that effect."

"Oh, Lizzy." Catherine swallowed back a sob. "I truly believed..." She shuddered. "He made unwelcome advances in the carriage, you see."

Elizabeth struggled to maintain her composure, her anger threatening to consume her. She yearned to flee the confines of the room, to pursue Wickham and deliver him his rightful retribution. The violent intensity of her wrath alarmed her.

"Did he harm you, dearest?" Her voice remained deceptively serene, masking the storm brewing within her.

"No," Kitty replied, a blend of malice and satisfaction underscoring her words. "I delivered a swift blow to his most vulnerable region, rendering him motionless." Another shudder coursed through her. "He possessed a note and money. I relieved him of both." A wicked little smile graced her lips. "I declare he shall have difficulty explaining to the coachman the whereabouts of his payment."

Elizabeth leaned down, enveloping her sister in a comforting embrace. "You displayed remarkable bravery, Kitty. Never allow anyone to tell you otherwise."

"Those poor girls," Kitty whispered. "The ones who perished." She shuddered once more, biting her trembling lip. "I believe he perpetrated similar acts upon them." Her voice wavered. "He was an entirely different man, Lizzy, as though everything I thought I knew was but a superficial façade he had assumed."

The notion sent a chilling cascade down Elizabeth's spine. To think that her sister had come perilously close to such a fate! It was no wonder Kitty was so shaken.

"And you walked all the way here?" she managed to inquire, her voice belying a calmness that masked her inner turmoil.

Catherine nodded weakly, her pale countenance receding further. "I travelled under the veil of night, seeking shelter during daylight hours," she murmured, her eyes drifting closed. "Lizzy..."

"Yes, dearest?"

"Could you please arrange for someone to bring me some food?" Her voice faded to a mere whisper. "I have gone without nourishment for... two days, I believe?"

"Of course." Relief washed over Lizzy at the prospect of momentarily leaving the room. Her thoughts were still in disarray, uncertain how to make sense of it all. Yet, she could not help but be grateful that Kitty had returned unharmed, with some hope of her reputation surviving intact.

*∧*∧*

To Elizabeth's immense relief, her sister's return went unmentioned, and Hill, bless her heart, refrained from imparting any tidbits of Meryton gossip—particularly concerning Kitty. However, the grapevine hummed with tales of Wickham's escapades. The cunning beast had apparently deserted his regiment, leaving behind a mountain of debts amounting to several hundred pounds.

Even more astonishing was the news that arrived three days hence. Mr Darcy, that enigmatic gentleman, had taken it upon himself to visit every shopkeeper in Meryton, meticulously ascertaining the extent of Wickham's financial entanglements and then, astonishingly, discharging each and every one of them from his own purse. Furthermore, Mr Darcy revealed that he had long been acquainted with Wickham, nurturing a hope, however, misplaced, that the man had mended his reckless ways —hence, his reticence in broadcasting the young reprobate's prior misdeeds to society's discerning ears.

Elizabeth found herself grateful that she and her sisters had been absent from Meryton during this tumultuous turn of events. In small villages, where lives exhibit little variance, the inhabitants possess an uncanny propensity for concocting elaborate speculations about any occurrence that disrupts their monotonous routines. Lizzy knew well that she could not have endured the ceaseless prattle any more than she could have borne the equally inevitable conjectures regarding her father's health.

Catherine, following her return, confined herself to her bedchamber for a span of two days. When she eventually ventured forth, she displayed a pallid countenance and an uncharacteristic air of restraint, frequently casting anxious glances towards her elder sisters as if beseeching them for reassurance. Her hours were largely spent in the company of her mother within Papa's chamber, only departing when the necessities of nature or her slumber compelled her.

During such circumstances, an unexpected visit from Miss Bingley proved to be both a welcome respite and a jolting surprise.

Within the south parlour, which felt disconcertingly vacant in the absence of her sisters and Mrs Bennet, Miss Bingley perched upon the very edge of the chaise lounge, her hands trembling and her head bowed.

"Miss Bingley?" Elizabeth endeavoured to infuse her voice with a semblance of warmth. "Pray, pardon the lacklustre reception and the disarray about us. Would you care for some tea?"

Miss Bingley raised her tear-streaked face, revealing a sallow complexion on one side, as if a blow had befallen her, and reddened, teary eyes.

"I implore you, do not trouble yourself," said she. "I am fully aware of my audacity in imposing upon your hospitality, but I simply could not endure... Oh, that wretched—forgive me, I ought not to speak ill of your aunt, yet—"

Elizabeth seated herself beside the distraught lady and tenderly took hold of her trembling hands. "To be honest, my sisters and I find it arduous to regard Lady Catherine as our aunt." She paused, contemplating the most effective means of soothing Caroline, who seemed oblivious to the identity of her confidante, seeking comfort in the understanding of a sympathetic fellow woman. "I understand that she, too, experiences difficulties adjusting to her altered circumstances."

A mirthless, bitter laughter escaped Miss Bingley's lips. "Indeed! She incessantly raves about those 'fortune-chasing harlots' who have purportedly duped her dear Anne into seclusion, hiding away in her chamber to escape the harangues."

Elizabeth could well fathom such a predicament. "And as the hostess, you are unable to seek solace there?"

Another bout of strained laughter erupted from Caroline's lips. "Alas, no. She deemed me a title-seeking social climber, Miss Eliza, and issued a mandate for me to steer clear of her nephews. She issued orders as though I were a mere servant!"

"I dare say Lady Catherine is accustomed to her every whim being heeded down to the minutest detail," offered Elizabeth, striving to maintain a neutral stance amid the tumultuous conversation.

"Detestable creature!" Miss Bingley's pent-up indignation and resentment burst forth in a torrent. "I am no servant to be commanded and directed according to her caprices! She referred to me as a tradesman's daughter and a shallow, insincere coquette, only to strike me when I retorted that I am a gentleman's sister, and she, a gentleman's wife—thus making us equals." The anger subsided, replaced by heart-wrenching sobs.

Elizabeth remained silent, for she could find no words adequate for such a situation. She simply embraced Miss Bingley, offering a comforting presence amidst the torrents of sorrow. She marvelled at the fact that the delicate balance of the Netherfield party had not already shattered under the strain of such profound tensions between its members.

A considerable interval transpired before Caroline regained her composure and withdrew herself. She mustered a melancholy chuckle. "I must appear a perfect simpleton, Miss Eliza."

"Pray, Miss Bingley," spoke Elizabeth in a gentle tone, "address me as Lizzy. It is the appellation bestowed upon me by all my esteemed companions." A smile graced her countenance. "You do not appear foolish in my eyes. Lady Catherine's unwarranted castigation of your person was unworthy."

"Then you must refer to me as Caro, as Louisa does." This simple declaration revealed a great deal to Elizabeth about the dearth of Miss Bingley's friendships—or rather, the absence thereof.

"I would be honoured." She extended a handkerchief to her companion. "Here. Your handkerchief must be thoroughly dishevelled by now."

"Oh!" Caroline blushed, then offered a tentative smile. "Indeed, it is quite damp." She delicately dabbed at her eyes but soon forsook such gentility and wiped her eyes properly before resorting to blowing her nose. "I apologise. Now I have rendered yours unsightly."

Elizabeth emitted a soft laugh. "It is of no consequence, Miss... Caro. We have been laundering handkerchiefs with great frequency as of late."

This remark elicited a startled glance, followed by a more contemplative one. "Miss... Lizzy? May I pose a terribly selfish question to you?"

"Of course." Elizabeth took care to maintain a soothing, soft tone. "Yet I implore you to grant me the prerogative of determining its degree of selfishness."

Caroline blinked, clearly attempting to hold back further tears. "I... am I lacking refinement?"

Lady Catherine must have been in a most vexing disposition, Elizabeth mused. "Absolutely not." The worst that could be ascribed to Miss Bingley was an excessive preoccupation with decorum and shallowness—a failing commonly found among young ladies, given the absence of alternative models.

Caroline shuddered. "It... You see, Papa sent me to a fashionable finishing school, and the young ladies there were cruel, all because he amassed his fortune through trade." She uttered the final word with a distasteful sneer.

"Which only evinces a lack of manners and restraint on their part," stated Elizabeth in a crisp tone that could have emanated from the throat of Mrs Bennet. "The true measure of a man lies not in how he treats his equals or superiors, but in how he treats those he regards as inferior."

Caroline appeared pensive; her lip caught between her teeth. "Mr Darcy never fails to exhibit politeness, even towards the lowliest of servants."

"Indeed." Lizzy smiled to temper her words.

For a moment, it seemed that Caroline would succumb to a fresh bout of tears. Yet she swallowed, blinked several times, and employed the now sodden handkerchief to dry her eyes. "You appear remarkably sagacious... I was a fool not to discern it." She shook her head. "Lady Catherine opines that Mr Darcy shall unite with Miss De Bourgh, but—" More tears welled.

Initially perplexed as to why Lady Catherine insisted on her daughter's matrimonial prospects would provoke tears from Miss Bingley, Elizabeth swiftly castigated herself for failing to realise the lady's excessive deference towards Mr Darcy constituted a polite means of ingratiating herself with the gentleman. She herself had cared not a whit for Mr Darcy's good opinion and, as a result, had engaged in challenges and teasing, thereby fostering a sort of friendship between them. "Do you harbour affection for Mr Darcy?" inquired she.

"I... I know not," Caroline replied, punctuated by a sorrowful laugh. She lowered her head. "I confess, I comprehend so little of his discourse. He possesses a peculiar manner concerning societal affairs. How foolish it sounds."

Elizabeth smiled. "Would you desire to spend the entirety of your existence with a man whom you fail to understand?" She carefully maintained a neutral tone, even as she marvelled at the twist of fate that placed her in this role. Certainly, since Lizzy and her sisters had been revealed as the nieces of the Earl of Ashton, they had ascended in Miss Bingley's and Mrs Hurst's estimation. However, for Caroline Bingley to seek Elizabeth Bennet out as a confidante was quite unforeseen.

No, Caroline had merely sought a sympathetic ear. The subsequent developments had transpired because Elizabeth had listened without condemnation.

"Oh!" Miss Bingley straightened, a hand rising to her mouth. "I have been lamenting my own misfortunes without a single inquiry regarding your family. Lizzy, I beg your pardon." She swallowed. "How fares Mr Bennet? And your sister, Catherine?"

Elizabeth stood and offered a smile. "Papa remains stable, though he slumbers extensively and does not always recognise us. Catherine is recuperating admirably."

"Please convey my regards to them." Caroline sounded almost humble. "I pray for their swift restoration to full health."

"Thank you."

*∧*∧*

Lady Catherine, in spite of her aversion to confessing

vulnerability, found herself compelled to acknowledge her fear within the confines of her chamber at Netherfield. Indeed, she could not deny that terror had taken hold of her if she were honest with herself.

She had anticipated that once she bestowed upon that vile creature, the elder Mr Darcy had inexplicably favoured, a sufficient sum of wealth and loaned him her carriage to tarnish the reputation of those fortune-seeking Bennet women, she would be rid of him forever.

Yet, to her dismay, she discovered the impertinent wretch awaiting her in her sanctuary, bearing the marks of a brawl, dishevelled and alarmingly furious.

Such insolence was unfamiliar to Lady Catherine, who struggled to restrain her tongue. Only her fear provided her with the strength to do so, though she abhorred the weakness that compelled her to hold back her true sentiments for such an individual. There were no words vile enough to describe him adequately.

He, however, imposed no such restraint upon himself. Lady Catherine remained oblivious to the full meaning of his vehement diatribe, though she was certain that its content was unsuitable for delicate ears. However, what she could gather appalled her.

"I instructed you to compromise and disgrace the girl, not abduct her." The ramifications if anyone were to discover her involvement in this debacle!

The retort she received left no doubt as to his opinion. "And do it all for the trifling sum you offered? No, madam. I shall not allow that to befall me."

Involuntarily, Lady Catherine took a step backwards. "You should be grateful for your failure," she retorted with as much dignity as she could muster. "Otherwise, you would be compelled to remedy your mounting debts as well."

The man flushed, his hands clenching tightly. Evidently,

he was well aware that news of Lieutenant Wickham's accumulating debts had spread from Meryton to the surrounding villages and that the militia was in pursuit of him. "Perhaps."

Something in his tone sent a chill akin to ice water coursing down Lady Catherine's spine. Surely this scoundrel did not expect her compliance, but he was here, in her chamber. She retreated another step.

"You see, the little harlot has escaped, along with your letter to your acquaintance in London, the one that recommended me as a helpful accomplice."

Lady Catherine felt the blood drain from her face. Even if she were to claim coercion should the letter be revealed, her reputation would forever be tainted. This was unbearable. "So you come to threaten me?" she demanded with more bravery than she truly felt.

He sneered. "I need not do anything, madam. By now, the girl is undoubtedly reunited with her family." His eyes narrowed. "Though, if you desire the problem to be eradicated, for a suitable recompense, that can be arranged."

# Chapter 12

Mr Bennet found himself enveloped in a realm of dreams, with fleeting recollections of a note from Kitty and an oppressive weight on his chest, yet everything else was a jumble of confusion. He was overcome with fatigue to the point that, even when he endeavoured to remain awake, he found himself slipping back into the embrace of dreams.

Amidst those dreams, he discerned various voices, each comforting in its own way, soothing him as he traversed the threshold between fragmented consciousness and genuine slumber. Mrs Bennet, Jane, Lizzy, Mary, Lydia and Kitty. Yet, it was impossible, for Kitty had eloped with Lieutenant Wickham, and Mrs Bennet would not spend so much time at his sickbed. Surely, those voices must be figments of his imagination.

And yet, when he finally emerged from the depths of weariness and the weight pressing upon him subsided, Mr Bennet discovered his wife seated in a wing-backed chair, pulled close to his bedside, her head resting against one of its wings as she dozed. There was a softness to her countenance in slumber, a stark contrast to her usual severity.

Not that Mr Bennet would ever deem Mrs Bennet a beauty, but she appeared far less formidable with her hair cascading loosely and her features relaxed in sleep, more reminding him of the woman he had married those sixteen years back.

The man attempted to rise, only to find himself lacking the

strength to do so.

Startled awake, Mrs Bennet scrutinised him intently for a moment before a smile of pure delight transformed her austere features. "It is a relief to have you back amongst us, sir. Shall I summon assistance to aid you in attending to your needs?"

"That would be greatly appreciated," replied he, his voice sounding feeble even to his own ears. How long had he been confined to his bed? And, perhaps more disconcertingly, who had tended to those tasks one typically performed for oneself during that time? Surely not his daughters or his wife herself.

The arrival of Mr Hill and his son, Jason—the eldest boy— interrupted any further contemplation on the matter. Mr Bennet exerted all his concentration to direct his uncooperative limbs and maintain his balance.

Once the necessities were attended to, and he was reclining in bed, propped up by an arrangement of cushions, the two men took their leave, assuring him that a warm broth would be brought shortly. The palpable relief in their countenances hinted at the gravity of his condition. Mr Bennet winced at the thought of the trouble he must have caused.

"Dare I inquire as to what manner of madness has befallen this household of late?" queried he, his voice sounding frail.

An enigmatic smile touched Mrs Bennet's lips. "Every possible sort of madness, sir," she replied in a wry tone. "Kitty has returned unharmed, though it seems the scoundrel did not fare as well. Those who observed her absence from Meryton have been led to believe it was due to her illness. They remain unaware of the true circumstances."

A wave of relief washed over him. There would be no disgrace to hinder his other daughters' marriage prospects.

"The scoundrel's debts have become the talk of the village," continued Mrs Bennet. "Regrettably, your health has been overshadowed by more intriguing gossip."

Mr Bennet could not help but smile. "I must confess great

disappointment. Is it not my duty in society to provide fodder for idle minds?" He acknowledged that he would prefer such speculation to revolve around matters other than his imminent demise, but that was a realm over which he held little control.

Returning his smile, the lady remarked, "Oh, I imagine your status shall be restored once it becomes known that I faithfully sat by your bedside for over a week."

Had it truly been so long? Mr Bennet could not recall. Time seemed to have eluded him entirely.

Instead of dwelling on the severity of his illness, he turned his attention to his wife's admission. "I have not deserved such kindness from you, Mrs Bennet," said he, struggling to speak. "I just now realised how a poor husband I have been to you all those years, never appreciating your goodness and intelligence." He noticed a radiance about her that he had seen those years back when they had shared more than living in the same household.

"That is very kind of you to say, sir," replied she.

"Oh, no," the man smiled. "It is selfish of me, for I do not wish to spend the rest of my life within the walls of my library and feel lonely when our daughters get married."

Mrs Bennet blinked and wiped her eyes with her sleeve, a behaviour she would never have allowed her daughters to exhibit. She then reached forward to clasp his hand. "If that is selfishness, then I am guilty of the same sin."

*∧*∧*

Darcy paced to and fro within the confines of Netherfield's well-stocked library, intermittently casting disapproving glances at the sombre mist and the constant drizzle that beset the landscape beyond the windowpanes. It seemed as though the entire world had conspired to vex and confound him.

To be cooped up indoors when his heart longed for an

invigorating ride across the countryside, with the fortuitous possibility of stumbling upon Longbourn, was a grievous plight in itself. The recent cessation of Wickham's assaults had undoubtedly confirmed him as the miscreant, prompting Darcy to question whether he could have averted such calamities and shudder at the peril his sister had narrowly escaped by avoiding an elopement with that rogue.

The gradual convalescence of Mr Bennet had dispelled the gloom that had enshrouded Longbourn. Now that the gentleman had regained enough strength to venture downstairs to his sanctuary of books, Darcy had resumed his frequent visits. Many of these encounters transpired over the chessboard, with several engaging matches against the captivating Miss Elizabeth herself, who displayed a mastery of the game that rivalled, if not surpassed, even her esteemed father's skill.

Though Darcy was acknowledged as one of the superior players within his social circle, he found himself compelled to exert utmost acuity to overcome either of the Bennets—a task rendered far from facile by Miss Elizabeth's enchanting laughter and beguiling smiles.

He sincerely desired to liberate Anne from the clutches of her mother's tyranny, for she had often spoken longingly of her brief visit to Longbourn. Curiously, of late, Miss Bingley had taken upon herself the role of Anne's frequent visitor, deftly eluding the watchful eye of Aunt Catherine. When Bingley had questioned her motives, she had claimed it as her duty as hostess to ensure the comfort of all her guests. Yet, there lingered an air of subtle alteration in her comportment, an almost diffident disposition.

Indeed, Anne derived great pleasure from Miss Bingley's calls —Darcy had borne witness to their shared laughter on more than one occasion. Moreover, Miss Bingley's laughter seemed unfeigned and significantly more pleasing to his ears than what he had grown accustomed to hearing from her.

Her attitude towards him had undergone a similarly

dramatic transformation, too. Instead of the overt, obsequious deference commonly exhibited by well-bred young ladies eager to ensnare a suitable husband, she now treated him as a mere acquaintance, someone whose company she genuinely enjoyed.

Darcy was forced to concede that Caroline Bingley proved far more agreeable when she was not overtly pursuing him, though he remained sceptical that she had entirely relinquished her designs. Surely a reproof from Aunt Catherine—something scarcely evaded by those acquainted with his aunt's character—could not have wrought such a marked alteration.

He would have sought an explanation were it not for the apprehension that any attention from him would provoke a resurgence of the excessive deference that left him feeling akin to a hunted creature. Unlike Bingley, he lacked the innate ability to feel at ease in social gatherings, particularly amongst those with whom he had limited acquaintance. This deficiency was a severe shortcoming for a young man of fortune, yet no matter what Darcy attempted, he found no solace in alleviating his discomfort.

Returning to Pemberley after his father's demise had offered a respite in many respects. There, he had been spared the torment of nausea that plagued him during every social occasion. He was no longer compelled to defend himself against the advances of predatory young ladies who would not hesitate to ensnare him in compromising situations, all in the hopes of securing the title of Mrs Darcy.

Perhaps it was precisely this that intrigued him so about Miss Elizabeth. Never once did she impose her company upon him, nor did she exhibit deference unless it concerned a matter in which he possessed superior expertise—an exceptional quality indeed.

Sighing deeply, he once again directed his gaze towards the window, still hoping that a ride might quell the restlessness that consumed him. Idleness sat uneasily upon his shoulders, and he found himself adrift within the confines of

Netherfield. At Pemberley, there had always been a plethora of improvements to be contemplated, visits to tenants, and, on occasion, even assisting in the repairs of their humble abodes or outbuildings—a rarity, given his father's teachings on the value of regular maintenance in averting major repairs, barring natural disasters. When inclement weather prevented outdoor ventures, there was the perpetual management of Pemberley to occupy his time, not to mention the joys of discussing music with Georgiana or indulging in shared reading sessions in the library.

Another weary sigh escaped Darcy's lips. He yearned for those pleasant moments with Georgiana, and he pined for the comforts of his ancestral home. Yet, he could not bring himself to depart. Miss Elizabeth had transformed this otherwise unremarkable corner of Hertfordshire into a veritable paradise, but only when enlivened by her presence.

Worse still, he was plagued by the most wretched form of cowardice—an incapacity to summon the courage necessary to request permission from the lady to court her, to embark upon a delightful path that might lead to the ultimate union between them.

*∧*∧*

After five rain-laden days, Lizzy, in the company of Kitty and Lydia, embarked on a brisk saunter towards Oakham Mount. Aware of the inevitability of mud besmirching their skirts, all three sisters donned older garments, with Elizabeth arming herself habitually with a flintlock. Not that she anticipated any troubles along their path; however, the reassuring heft of the weapon provided her with solace.

The woods, invigorated by the recent downpour, appeared to exude a newfound freshness. Verdant foliage flourished, and vibrant wildflowers bestowed their blooms upon the landscape.

The sisters seized every opportunity to gather wild herbs during their ramble, with Elizabeth's basket swiftly becoming laden with verdure while Kitty and Lydia carried fragrant posies.

As the path grew steeper, Kitty voiced her melancholy sentiment, "I shall miss this." She sighed. "Jane will soon depart for Rosings, being the heiress and all. I dare say I was happier when our birth Mama was just that, a Mama."

"Indeed!" Lydia left no room for doubt regarding her opinion. "This alteration in fortune only begets more trouble than it is worth." Though a change of fortune had little to do with her, as she had been the only one not related to the new noble family, she had preferred the simple life they all once had shared.

Kitty's countenance turned grave, undoubtedly recalling her perilous brush with disgrace and its potential consequences.

Though inclined to concur, Elizabeth could not allow her sisters to view their newfound circumstances through such a desolate prism. "Ah, but envision the uncharted realms we may explore in the company of the newfound relatives," she endeavoured to say with as much cheerfulness as she could muster. "Rosings Park must hold splendid gardens and untamed wildernesses where we may roam. And I have reason to believe the houses of our new cousins are equally charming." Unable to resist a playful addition, she quipped, "Furthermore, Papa may yearn for some private moments with Mama."

Kitty emitted a soft laugh. "Oh, Lizzy! That is truly wicked! However, Mama and Papa deserve a honeymoon. I do not suppose they had one before, having four and a while later, five little children to rise. And I also dare not to presume they were as in love as they are now."

"Indeed," Lydia assented, her cheeks blushing.

Elizabeth bestowed a gentle smile upon her sisters. "You see, there is goodness amidst the adversity. Undoubtedly, we shall adapt. Besides, I suspect we would have been separated soon, regardless. Mr Collins is pursuing Mary's affections, and if Mr

Bingley does not imminently solicit Jane's hand, I shall declare myself blind."

Catherine sighed wistfully. "If only it were not necessary for families to scatter in so many divergent directions."

Lydia giggled. "Yes, but picture all of us and our spouses congregating in Longbourn. What a tumultuous affair! We would drive poor Hill to the brink of insanity."

"Indeed, you mean poor Papa," countered Kitty. "He despises overcrowding, retreating to his library and barricading the door."

Suppressing a frown, Elizabeth detected an unsettling disquiet in the woods. The birds seemed excessively hushed, and shadows took on an uncanny nature. Adjusting her basket to ensure easy access to her flintlock, Lizzy hoped that her unease was mere fancy.

"Ah, but Papa would never dream of locking Mama out," declared Lydia, shaking her head. "No, he would establish a cosy encampment for both of them within the confines of the library."

"And there, by the soft glow of candlelight, they would indulge in literary pursuits," Kitty blushed, her thoughts straying towards more intimate activities hinted at by her words.

"Meanwhile, Hill would deliver meals to them through the windows," Lydia added mischievously. "And though it would scandalise the gossips, their newfound love would render such trifles inconsequential."

Both girls erupted into laughter, and Elizabeth joined in, though her mind remained preoccupied.

"How peculiar it shall be," mused Lydia, her cheerfulness giving way to contemplation. "I can hardly fathom Longbourn without Jane. She possesses an unrivalled serenity."

"Oh, yes. I shall miss Jane when she—" Kitty's words were abruptly drowned out by the resounding blast of a gunshot, a thunderclap that pierced the air. Her piercing scream confronted the tranquillity of the surroundings.

Elizabeth swiftly twirled towards her sister, just in the nick of time to catch her sister as she collapsed. Kitty grasped desperately at her side, where crimson stained her trembling hand.

Unwilling to fuss over finding material for a bandage, Lizzy promptly shed her jacket and applied it to the wound once she and Lydia had safely lowered Kitty to the ground.

"How remarkably touching," remarked Wickham, though his tone carried an unsettling discord. Being positioned behind them, he could not behold Elizabet's concealed basket. She deftly sought the grip of the flintlock within, wrapping her fingers around it, instinctively finding the trigger.

"Save your sneers for a more suitable target," she retorted, her words dripping with defiance.

"He possesses another firearm," Lydia whispered, her voice barely audible.

Yet a fragment of Elizabeth's consciousness remained detached and composed. If Wickham possessed an additional weapon, she must seize the element of surprise and discharge her shot first. However, there existed the grim prospect that he might inflict harm upon her or Lydia. "Prepare to seek aid swiftly," she responded, carefully withdrawing the flintlock.

Lydia's eyes grew wide, her countenance filled with trepidation. Yet she nodded, acknowledging the plan.

"Rise, both of you, and pivot so that I may lay eyes upon you," demanded the man.

"Merely to revel in your triumph? I had not deemed you so bland." Lizzy regained her footing, meticulously prolonging her ascent to maintain her equilibrium. She knew she possessed only one opportunity.

"Silence!" The jeers noticeably unsettled Wickham, evidently unprepared for such resolute audacity.

Elizabeth had no intention of gratifying his expectations by cowering in fear, regardless of the terror that coursed through her veins.

Before she could reconsider, she pivoted, her hand clutching the concealed flintlock beneath her gown.

Wickham stood a mere twenty feet away, a pistol grasped in each hand, one directed at her, the other at Lydia.

His smile twisted in a manner that sent a surge of discomfort through Lizzy's abdomen. Finally, she comprehended what Kitty had witnessed. That was the genuine Wickham, devoid of the veneer of charm and civility.

Raising her flintlock, she fired.

Wickham's firearms resounded.

It seemed as if time itself halted as he staggered backwards, the man's visage transformed into a mangled mass of shattered flesh. He emitted no cry of agony.

Elizabeth advanced a few steps toward him, now lying in agony, gasping for breath. Both of his pistols had discharged two rounds each. She lifted each one, electing the weightier of the two. It resembled nought, but subduing a raging bull, she reassured herself until her trembling hands steadied.

This time, she took deliberate aim. Wickham, so grievously injured, could not endure. This was an act of mercy. It could be nought else.

She fired.

Wickham's body convulsed in a solitary spasm, then became utterly motionless.

Elizabeth allowed the gun to slip from her grasp. All vigour seemed to have abandoned her frame; she could not fathom her next course of action. She had ended a man's life —a transgression punishable by hanging or transportation if fortune favoured her.

"Lizzy?" Lydia's voice appeared distant, tinged with fear.

"Lizzy, your arm!"

# Chapter 13

His two cousins and Bingley shared Darcy's longing for the outdoors, as the atmosphere at Netherfield was too restrictive, and the Colonel had lost his best reason to stay with the imminent departure of the militia to Brighton. Therefore, they all were out riding without a clear destination, though Darcy suspected—or better hoped—they would eventually end up at Longbourn, where Miss Bennets were a significant attraction. For now, the woods around Oakham Mount were pleasant, and there was always the chance they would run into the young ladies on one of their frequent walks on a beautiful day like this.

Suddenly, a single gunshot pierced the tranquil atmosphere, followed by a blood-curdling scream.

Darcy urged his horse towards the commotion, realising belatedly that his three companions shared the same instinctive response. They raced towards the mount, only to be compelled to rein in their steeds as the sound of multiple gunshots reverberated nearby.

Once he had composed his mount, Darcy alighted from his steed, adroitly securing the reins around the nearest branch, and hastened towards the source of the shots, lamenting the absence of any weapon other than his bare hands.

He froze at the sight that awaited him—Miss Elizabeth Bennet, standing over a mortally wounded man. Her sleeve bore a stain of deep red, though she seemed oblivious to it, her countenance an inscrutable mask.

Adjacent to her lay Miss Catherine Bennet, her sister Lydia torn between aiding one sibling or the other, her indecision palpable.

Elizabeth raised the pistol, poised it meticulously, and discharged a fatal shot into the man's chest.

A realisation dawned upon Darcy; it was an act of mercy. The man's visage was marred beyond redemption, rendering survival an impossibility, albeit he might have languished for several days in excruciating agony before succumbing.

Elizabeth relinquished her hold on the firearm; her body convulsed with tremors.

Lydia glanced between her two sisters, beseeching guidance. "Lizzy, your arm!"

Darcy compelled himself to advance. Whatever untoward deed Elizabeth had perpetrated, and its reason could be deferred until the injured sisters received proper care and assistance.

Elizabeth turned, her movements lacking their customary grace. At first, she appeared oblivious to his presence, but upon the realisation that she and her sisters were no longer alone, her countenance drained of colour, and her equilibrium wavered precariously.

Acting swiftly, Darcy caught her, ensuring her injured arm remained undisturbed. Though she did not faint, she allowed him to guide her wordlessly towards her sisters.

"Oh, thank heavens thou hast discovered us!" Lydia hastened to assist Darcy in gently settling Elizabeth against the sturdy trunk of a tree. "It was Wickham. He hath fired upon Kitty, and he would have killed us had not Lizzy intervened. She must not let be hang for it!"

Good God! It is no wonder that Elizabeth findeth herself in such a discomposed state. To take a man's life in defence of her sisters—and her own person—and then to face the spectre of the hangman's noose for her noble actions?

Darcy shook his head. "I shall take care of this matter; fear not, Miss Lydia. Now, look after your sisters until I can bring help."

Lydia raised her tear-stained countenance to meet his gaze. "I am grateful, Mr Darcy. I shall endeavour to do what little I can."

He turned then, confronting the bewildered countenances of his cousins. Bingley appeared as though he might succumb to a fit of illness. However, it was hardly surprising considering Bingley's lack of military experience, unlike Fitzwilliams, who had served actively in the army.

"Charles, make haste to Longbourn and inform Mr Bennet that we happened upon Wickham, who threatened his daughters and was ultimately dispatched by our hands, though not before he inflicted wounds upon Miss Elizabeth and Miss Catherine. Instruct Bennet to summon the authorities to dispose of Wickham's remains and inform him that we shall speedily return his daughters home. Bring back bandages and anything else necessary."

Bingley nodded and swallowed, then hastened towards his horse.

Both Fitzwilliams expressed their approbation of Darcy's quick actions.

Randall wore a wry smile. "Pray tell, which one of us delivered the fatal blow?"

"I discharged one shot," replied Darcy without hesitation. "Richard, would you like to have the honour of the second? We cannot ascertain with certainty which of us delivered the fatal stroke."

"Indeed." The Colonel appeared to find this notion rather amusing. "In circumstances such as these, when a rogue is poised to harm young ladies, one acts upon instinct."

Lydia emitted a strange sound resembling a sob.

"Fear not, Miss Lydia," uttered Randall soothingly. "The

ordeal is over. No one shall meet the hangman's noose; we shall ensure that." He knelt beside Catherine and applied additional pressure, his coat serving as an impromptu bandage. "Have you anything to stop the bleeding?"

Lydia secured a strip of cloth, likely torn from her petticoat, around Elizabeth's injured arm.

"We have gathered some herbs, though their efficacy pales in comparison to a salve."

Darcy occupied himself arranging the weapons, claiming the flintlock for himself and proffering one of the two-shot pistols to the Colonel. The remaining pistol he positioned beside Wickham's right hand as though it had fallen there.

"That should suffice, cousin," Fitzwilliam asserted, his countenance displaying a grim smile. "Our narrative would prove credible even if the ladies were found in possession of the firearms."

"It is best to dispel any doubt," Darcy reminded him. "Though I must remark that Miss Elizabeth's bravery and fortitude of mind should be extolled, not concealed in this manner."

The Colonel shook his head. "Truly, that is the voice of a man violently in love."

"For heaven's sake, Richard! Miss Elizabeth possesses neither impaired hearing nor unconsciousness."

Darcy inwardly chided himself for the blush that threatened to grace his cheeks. How embarrassing it would be to display the blush of a guilty child while reciting falsehoods to safeguard the lady's reputation.

Elizabeth's soft laughter did nought to steady his composure. "Indeed, Colonel," she interjected with a voice lacking firmness. "Grant Mr Darcy the opportunity to declare himself before sentencing him to such a dire fate."

"Lizzy, you must be still!" Lydia's voice trembled with desperation. "You must refrain from moving the injured arm."

"Should I instead yield to a decorous swoon?" Elizabeth queried.

Darcy avoided looking in that direction and focused on hiding any traces of Miss Bennets' presence near the dead man.

Lydia asked for help identifying a salve for bleeding, and Lizzy attempted to stand up but was stopped by Lord Fitzwilliam. Fortunately, the sound of approaching hoofbeats signalled Bingley's arrival with assistance. He came running into the clearing, followed by a middle-aged man carrying a basket of bandages and salves.

*∧*∧*

No inquiries were raised by any of the gentlemen when Mr Darcy and his cousins recounted the events. However he felt unease in being showered with praise for their presumed heroism, he deemed it preferable to endure such honours rather than jeopardise Miss Elizabeth's reputation.

It was not until he had escorted Mr Bennet and his daughters to Longbourn, seeing Misses Catherine and Elizabeth being assisted to their chambers and the arrival of the attending physician, that Darcy discovered the extent of his misconception.

Once he and Mr Bennet found themselves alone in the hallway, the older gentleman spoke gravely, saying, "Let us retire to the library, young man, where you may divulge the true account."

After fortifying himself with a sip of brandy, Darcy found the genuine narrative far more effortless to convey than the fabrications he had concocted for Elizabeth's sake.

"Hmm," mused Mr Bennet with a furrowed brow. "Fascinating. Were you aware of this?" He handed Darcy a well-worn letter.

As if the shocking nature of Lady Catherine's penmanship

was not enough, the missive contents compelled him to consume the remaining brandy in one gulp. "Good God," uttered he.

"You cannot fathom the relief that washes over me upon hearing your shock," remarked Mr Bennet, his tone returning to its customary dryness. "It helps the information I received earlier today far easier to disclose."

Darcy felt the blood draining from his face. "Do you possess evidence implicating my aunt in this... endeavour?" The scandal had the potential to ruin not only his entire family but also Bennets. However, the revelation of Lady Catherine's conspiracy to commit murder required the pursuit of justice, even if it remained confidential.

Bennet sighed and closed his eyes. "Indeed, I do. Bingley arrived as I was organising a party to locate my daughters and bring them home. A party heavily armed, I might add."

Darcy winced. "It is fortunate that Miss Elizabeth possesses a courage and composure equal to the finest of men," he acknowledged. "Fitzwilliam is already lamenting his inability to claim her for the army."

A faint smile graced the countenance of the older man. "I dare say the army would prove an inadequate challenge for my Lizzy. No matter what instructions the doctor imparts, I expect to find her on her feet come to-morrow." He shook his head. "When she was but a child, her first words after 'Mama' and 'Papa' were: Lizzy do!"

In Darcy's mind, he envisioned a curly-haired toddler gazing up at her parents with those remarkable eyes and uttering, in a tone that brooked no disagreement, "Lizzy do!" He could readily imagine that child succeeding in any endeavour she pursued, no matter how improbable success might seem.

"You must be exceedingly proud, sir."

"Indeed," chuckled Bennet softly. "Had she been a boy, there would have been no restraining her."

Darcy nodded, then swallowed hard. "I ought to return to Netherfield. This matter—I must inform my uncle and cousins of it."

"Of course."

*∧*∧*

"What did she do?" The Earl's brow furrowed. "I understand Catherine can be overbearing, but I can scarcely believe she would engage in something so abhorrent."

Darcy simply handed him the letter. Mr Bennet had willingly relinquished it under the condition that it not be given to its author—a condition with which Darcy had wholeheartedly concurred.

The Earl's countenance grew increasingly furrowed, and his complexion deepened in hue as he perused the missive. Only after he finished reading did he return the damning document to his nephew before uttering a word. "And what of the... other matter?"

"Bingley and I have conducted interviews with the servants who were privy to these meetings," Darcy informed him. "I am convinced that their testimonies are sincere." He saw no need to divulge the specifics of those interviews.

The Earl's expletive could have easily been mistaken for one uttered by a stablehand. He sighed wearily. "Very well. I shall request your presence, along with my sons, when we address this matter with Catherine. I can only hope she exhibits some semblance of remorse for her imprudence."

Darcy nodded solemnly. "I shall be there. Bingley as well, if you so wish. We have discussed this matter thoroughly."

"I appreciate the offer," his lordship sighed once more. "Given that this transpired under his own roof, it is only fitting that Bingley be present."

Darcy understood his uncle's hesitance in dealing with the situation. Lady Catherine was his sister, after all.

"I understand that Wickham initially approached her, and his demeanour grew increasingly menacing with each encounter." It offered little solace: Aunt Catherine could have confided in any of her relatives. All of them were aware of Wickham's untrustworthiness, though none had comprehended the depths of the man's wickedness. "It is plausible that she felt sufficiently threatened to provide him with funds and feign approval of his actions."

Though a flicker of hope briefly illuminated the Earl's features, he shook his head. "Darcy, you are well aware that Catherine could have sought protection from any of us, and it would have been readily granted. I must admit, I cannot envision any explanation she could offer that absolves her of culpability."

Darcy shared the same sentiment, and he ardently wished for an alternative. The recollection of Elizabeth standing resolute over Wickham, her countenance devoid of emotion, as she delivered the final, merciful blow was disturbing, to say at least. She should never have been compelled to such extremities.

He wholeheartedly agreed with Bennet's assertion that, regardless of the doctor's prognosis, Elizabeth would undoubtedly rise the following morn, engaging herself in some purposeful pursuit.

It was almost regrettable that Aunt Catherine could not be placed under the care of Bennets. That family possessed an extraordinary capacity for miracles, adeptly transforming the woman's obsequious imitation of a clergyman into a sensible —and even amiable—man within a matter of weeks. Darcy suspected that one or more of Miss Bennets played a role in Miss Bingley's transformation as well.

In the library, she had orchestrated a deliberate encounter where she expressed regret for her past behaviour and conceded that while she would be honoured if he were to regard her as more than just the sister of his esteemed friend, she maintained reservations about the possibility of anything further blossoming between them.

Once Darcy had regained his composure and expressed his gratitude for Miss Bingley's forthrightness, he found her already making her retreat. It had been evident that Miss Bennets had influenced such a change in her demeanour, for she had visited Longbourn on more than one occasion.

Darcy hoped that Bingley had managed to convey his suggestion of including Anne in these visits. His delicate cousin would surely benefit from the transformative presence of the Bennet family, whose influence seemed nothing short of miraculous. However, he understood that the Bennets might not be ready to receive visitors at the moment. Miss Catherine's injury required her to remain in bed, and the potential for infection loomed, which could prove fatal.

Both Randall and Richard had witnessed men succumb to lesser injuries.

To Darcy's relief, his aunt displayed no apprehension about joining the family in Netherfield's second parlour, a cosy room intended for informal gatherings. Lady Fitzwilliam's presence undoubtedly assuaged any concerns Lady Catherine might have born.

They had spared Anne the distressing confrontation. She and Miss Bingley were engrossed in practising duets at the far end of the building—an activity suggested by Miss Bingley herself. It was not as if Anne remained oblivious to her mother's treachery. Darcy, along with the Fitzwilliam brothers, had insisted that their cousin deserved to know what was to transpire and the reasons behind it. Anne might be delicate, but she was far from unintelligent.

Lady Catherine cast a frigid glare at Bingley, silently accusing him of sullying the room with his presence.

Yet, uncharacteristically, she refrained from articulating such sentiments.

"Is there a matter that necessitates my attention, brother? You have attended to me only when circumstances demanded it."

"That is because you make your company disagreeable, sister," he responded evenly. "Randall, do assist your aunt in finding her seat."

The Viscount and his brother promptly came to her aid, simultaneously relieving her of the weighty cane she carried.

"I bear unsettling tidings, Catherine," the Earl continued. "It appears that Wickham attempted to murder two of your nieces this morning. The timely arrival of your nephews and Mr Bingley thwarted his nefarious plans."

The woman's countenance drained of colour. "That... monster!" Her hands clenched tightly onto the chair's arms. For an instant, Darcy fancied that her hands resembled claws.

"Regrettably, there is evidence suggesting your complicity," the Earl stated without any trace of emotion.

She leaned forward. "And do you trust the lies of that scoundrel over me?" she demanded. "I am deeply offended, brother."

"In actuality, 'that scoundrel' had no opportunity to utter a word," the Viscount dryly remarked. "Thanks to the sharpshooting skills of Darcy and Richard, he met his demise before any interrogation could take place, though, sadly, not before inflicting grievous wounds upon the young ladies."

"Then there can be no connection." Lady Catherine's assertive tone clashed with her grip on the chair's arms.

"There are witnesses who have seen you meeting with the man," the Earl responded.

She gasped sharply and shook her head. "Mere servants," she dismissively uttered. "One should not rely on the word of those from the lower classes."

Now a hint of disapproval tinged Lord Ashton's voice. "When their accounts align with the contents of a document in your own handwriting, sister, one would be wise to take heed."

His sister's reaction surprised everyone in the room. She appeared to retreat into herself, her demeanour shrinking. "Then it is concluded. I cannot claim to lament being rid of that vile creature, even if it means being implicated myself," whispered she. She closed her eyes as if seeking solace within.

"Only ensure the well-being of Anne," implored she, her voice strained.

Darcy swallowed hard, but his other aunt spoke up before he could find the appropriate words.

"Oh, Catherine, no one intends to pass judgment on you without due consideration. Will you not reveal the motives behind your writings?"

"I had thought it glaringly apparent," Lady Catherine replied, her voice brittle. "I do not accept these Bennet women."

"That much is evident, Aunt," interjected Darcy, his tone formal, in keeping with the gravity of the situation. "But what of Wickham? How did he manage to establish contact with you?"

She lifted her head and averted her gaze.

"By all means, woman! The man has duped us all. Set aside your pride for once!" cried the Earl, his vehemence and likely his language causing his sister to flinch.

However, she straightened herself and fixed him with a cold glare. "I shall not be an object of pity," she spat. "You treat me with contempt unless you require something from me. Yes, all of you." Her gaze softened slightly as she fixed her eyes on Darcy. "Though you, nephew, have at least shown courtesy, in spite of your refusal to care for Anne."

The man bowed deeply; the formality seemed more apt at this moment. "Madam, I have never denied my commitment to providing Anne with all the care I can offer, including respecting her desire to remain unmarried," he conceded, acknowledging his cousin's valid reasons to fear the institution of marriage. "However, if Wickham has also ensnared you in his schemes, then please grant us knowledge of it so that we may ensure no acquaintance of his possesses the means to trouble you or Anne further."

The thought of harm befalling her sole surviving child overwhelmed her ladyship's considerable self-control. Her eyes shimmered with unshed tears, yet she paid them no mind. "You shall see to it," stated she, more as a command than a request.

Darcy simply nodded in acquiescence.

"Very well," she resigned herself, her figure seeming to shrink once more. "It commenced shortly after your father's demise, Darcy. He demanded an outrageous sum, threatening to ruin Anne and me should I fail to comply."

Darcy sighed heavily. "He possessed—and now possesses no longer—a remarkable talent for such manipulation."

Lady Catherine shrugged ever so slightly. "His claim appeared plausible enough to sway the Ton, in spite of being a vicious falsehood. I acceded to his demands on the condition that he never trouble me again."

A condition that Wickham evidently chose to ignore. That much was evident.

"He revisited several times thereafter, though he had ceased bothering me for a number of years until recently," continued she. The woman chuckled hollowly, wrapping her shawl more tightly around her shoulders. "I had dared to hope that I had finally rid myself of him." Tears welled in her eyes as she blinked, yet she disregarded them. "I believed his plan was to elope with the girl—a scandalous act, to be sure, but ultimately harmless. He deceived me."

It came as no surprise. On numerous occasions, Wickham had deceived Darcy and his father enough to know the man's prodigious skill for falsehood. The world was undoubtedly better off without Wickham's presence.

After an extended interval of hushed stillness, Lady Catherine tentatively inquired, "And what of the young ladies? Are they to recover?"

"Miss Elizabeth shall undoubtedly regain her health. As for Miss Catherine, time will see. I intend to call Longbourn on the morrow to inquire about the well-being of both young ladies." Darcy's utterance maintained an air of composure, devoid of embellishment.

Upon receiving this reassurance, his aunt drew a tremulous breath, only to succumb to weeping: convulsive sobs of profound anguish.

Instead of embarrassing her by revealing her weakness, Darcy quietly made his way towards the door of the parlour. Everyone, except for Aunt Fitzwilliam, followed suit with careful and respectful movements. Even Richard seemed humbled.

"Eleanor shall manage the situation," declared the Earl in a lowered voice once they had distanced themselves sufficiently from the chamber to preclude any eavesdropping. "Catherine must retreat to a more secluded place. The Ashfield dower house should prove adequate." His countenance contorted into a grimace. "None shall dare accuse Ashfield Hall of residing in close proximity to the circles of Society."

Considering that his uncle's estate was situated several miles to the north of Darcy's own estate, he could not dispute the proposition. He cast a fleeting glance at his cousins.

Both men bore a sombre countenance, and the Colonel was the first to break the silence. "Fear not, Darcy. Though it pains me to abandon the delightful company in these environs—particularly whilst on leave—I possess the requisite connections to track down Wickham's accomplices and ensure they do not stir up further trouble." A grin emerged on his face. "Besides, your conspicuous presence would be most incongruous in the places I am bound to investigate."

Darcy executed a wry bow. "My dear cousin, that is solely because you are an irrepressible rogue. I marvel that the Home Office has not yet solicited your services."

"Perhaps they have, but I am constrained from disclosing such matters," the Colonel admonished, wagging his finger playfully. "Or perchance I am merely jesting."

Randall emitted a snort. "I would wager my fortune on the latter scenario rather than the former."

Colonel Richard Fitzwilliam winked mischievously. "I shall retire early, gentlemen. I intend to embark at daybreak."

# Chapter 14

Though her arm throbbed with excruciating pain, Elizabeth valiantly persisted in her endeavours the day after her injury. The doctor's admonitions for her to find repose proved insufficient to confine her within the confines of the house, and even that sole concession was granted merely due to her rapid exhaustion, preventing her from traversing more than a room's length without halting to seek respite.

With Mrs Bennet tending to Kitty, whose condition was far direr, Lizzy meandered from the sunlit parlour to her father's study and back, driven by an indomitable restlessness.

During her sojourn, having paused in the vestibule to regain some semblance of ease, Mr Darcy made his arrival accompanied by Mr Bingley and the Viscount.

The three gentlemen exchanged a combination of astonishment and amusement before Randall declared, "Well, cousin, you have indeed proven your case." He executed a bow in Elizabeth's direction. "Dearest cousin, our wayward relative Darcy insisted you would be up and about, heedless of the physician's counsel."

Elizabeth could not withhold a smile. "It appears that Mr Darcy has acquired an inordinate understanding of my disposition, sir."

Darcy bowed in response. "Madam, that does not vex me in the slightest." His countenance betrayed a conflict between concern and amusement. "However, you ought to be resting."

She emitted a soft chuckle. "I am indeed at rest. I remain entirely within these walls, with my wanderings confined to the well-trodden path linking Papa's study and the parlour."

A flicker of amusement played upon Darcy's lips.

Bingley, unable to suppress his curiosity any longer, inquired, "How fares Miss Catherine?"

"She is confined to her bed and beset by a fever." Lizzy saw no reason to veil the truth before these gentlemen. "Mama and Mrs Hill attend to her."

Upon witnessing the gravity etched upon the faces of all three gentlemen, Elizabeth appended, "There are no signs of infection. Mama surmises that the fever stems from the loss of blood."

The Viscount nodded thoughtfully. "That explanation does indeed seem plausible."

"Lizzy?" Mr Bennet's voice emanated from the vicinity of the library, heralding his appearance. Though somewhat diminished in a frame and relying on a cane for support, he retained a spirit of mirth wherever it might be found. "Why do you hold court in the foyer? Surely the parlour would prove more agreeable."

Swiftly, Lord Fitzwilliam assured the man that no impropriety had transpired, elucidating their recent arrival at the premises and their natural inclination to inquire after Miss Bennet's well-being and that of her sister.

Since Elizabeth's intended destination was none other than the library, the gentlemen gallantly escorted her to the room before Darcy ventured to broach the other subject of their visit.

"Richard has embarked upon a sojourn to the metropolis, aiming to unveil any confederates Wickham may have consorted with in this diabolical scheme and to ensure that they do not perpetuate any further disturbances," uttered he in a simple yet meaningful manner. "Yesterday, we had the opportunity to confer with Lady Catherine, and it appears that the miscreant had been ensnaring her in his deceptive snare for quite some time, menacing her and Anne."

Mr Bennet nodded sagely. "Pray, do pardon me if I fail to forgive the lady of her complicity in this affair readily," he declared in a calm and earnest voice, betraying his genuine ire. "Naturally, I shall not utter a word on the matter, but her injudicious actions have inflicted considerable harm upon my dear family."

"Indeed, sir." Darcy displayed no semblance of astonishment in response to the man's retort. "Lady Catherine shall be retiring to the dower house of Ashfield Hall house and shall remain under close guard," stated he. "I have undertaken the responsibility of overseeing Rosings until such time as Miss Bennet is able to take possession of the estate and attend to Anne's welfare."

"A sensible compromise," Mr Bennet concurred. "However, my daughters shall not venture to Ashfield Hall so long as the lady continues to reside in close proximity."

Lord Fitzwilliam gravely inclined his head. "Father anticipated as much. Lady Catherine is presently in a state of great distress, yet there remains a glimmer of hope that she may come to rue her ill-advised actions. Would you consider a change of heart if she were to extend her sincerest regrets?"

Mr Bennet's lips curled at the corners. Without a doubt, he found these peculiar negotiations to be a source of mirth. A tinge of dryness infused his voice as he replied, "Should the lady's apologies prove persuasive and my daughters display willingness, I might be inclined to reconsider."

"Your kindness is deeply appreciated, sir." The Viscount's tone bore unmistakable traces of relief. "I would abhor the notion of being estranged from my newfound cousins over this unfortunate turn of events."

As intended, his words elicited a chuckle from Bennet. "Rest assured, young man, you need not harbour such concerns. All other kinfolks of yours—and yours, Darcy—are wholeheartedly welcome to grace our humble abode whenever the inclination arises." He bestowed a mischievous twinkle upon Bingley. "The same invitation, of course, extends to you and your sisters—if they aspire to forge an acquaintance with us."

Bingley contrived to secure a moment alone with Jane, during which he humbly sought her hand, a proposition that she ecstatically embraced. The expression on Bingley's countenance upon his emergence from Mr Bennet's study left no doubt that the father had bestowed his blessing upon the union.

As Lydia and Mary extended their felicitations to Jane, Darcy and Mr Collins graciously grasped Bingley's hand, offering their heartfelt congratulations. At the same time, the Viscount warmly embraced him, cordially welcoming him into the fold.

Elizabeth surmised that there must have been something extraordinary in the atmosphere, for shortly thereafter, the mirthful accolades were directed towards Mary and Mr Collins, causing both of them to blush fervently and attempt to retreat from the limelight. The notion of a dual wedding was promptly dismissed by the pair, with Mr Collins asserting his incongruity in such a gathering and Mary declaring her unwillingness to mar Jane's triumphant glory for anything in the world.

Lord Fitzwilliam, Mr Bingley, Jane, and Lydia endeavoured to sway their decisions while Darcy, in his unobtrusive manner, settled himself beside Elizabeth. "This is quite the commotion," uttered he, gently.

"Indeed it is." 'Commotion' was not precisely the term she would have chosen, yet it sufficed. "But they are all so unequivocally elated. I find no reason to raise any objections."

He bestowed upon her a smile that caused a peculiar sensation to pervade Elizabeth's being—a sensation not akin to ailment but rather to pleasure. Before she could ponder the peculiarity of her sentiments, Darcy spoke once more.

"Miss Elizabeth, when I beheld you standing resolutely

against that scoundrel yesterday, I came to a profound realisation of how ardently I love and admire you." A blush tinged his countenance as he divulged his sentiments, and he inched nearer to her, only to retract and cast his gaze downwards. "I am aware that my merits may be deemed meagre —aside from the trifling matter of a handsome fortune and an opulent estate—but I would be both honoured and exhilarated if you would consent to grant me the privilege of courting you."

Elizabeth swallowed hard, her eyes now brimming with tears of sheer felicity. "You possess an abundance of admirable attributes, Mr Darcy, though they may not conform to the dictates of fashion." A note of derision seeped into her voice as she mentioned fashion. "There is only one thing that could heighten my happiness—and you have yet to make that request."

She was as playful as her father, jesting when a man had all but declared his love for her.

Fortunately, Mr Darcy seemed to grasp the meaning behind her response. He smiled, leaning forward once more and clasping her hands. "In that case, would you bestow upon me the inestimable privilege of becoming my wife, Elizabeth?"

She smiled, her throat constricting with overwhelming emotion, and nodded. Then, finding her voice, she murmured, "Unless there exists another Mr Darcy of whom I am blissfully unaware."

He chuckled softly. "None that I am cognizant of."

*∧*∧*

In spite of the apparent eagerness displayed by all three betrothed couples to partake in the delights of matrimony— and the subsequent addition of Lord Randall Fitzwilliam to the roster of imminent nuptials upon his proposal to Miss Caroline Bingley, an offer she readily accepted—the weddings were not to be held until the arrival of autumn. By that time, Catherine

Bennet had regained her vitality and could stand alongside Lydia and Georgiana Darcy—the latter having quickly formed a close bond with the Bennet sisters, much like her cousin Anne de Bourgh—as the radiant bridesmaids for these joyous occasions.

With her mother absent from the scene and frequent visits to Longbourn lending her a helping hand, Anne's health had begun its gradual ascent towards restoration. It was the shared belief of all parties concerned that Anne would forever remain delicate, but her cheeks now boasted a touch of colour, and her countenance was adorned with frequent smiles—a triumph, as perceived by all her cousins.

The accounts of Anne's ameliorated health seemed to have a mollifying effect on the letters dispatched from Ashfield Dower House. Though immediate reconciliation remained improbable, the prospect of an eventual reunion grew brighter as the months preceding the weddings unfolded.

It was decided that Bingley and Jane would postpone their occupation of Rosings Park until after their honeymoon, to be spent in the tranquillity of Netherfield, for the Earl and Countess had returned to Ashfield, the Viscount to his own house, Darcy to Pemberley, and the Colonel to his military duties.

Following the nuptial celebrations, Mr and Mrs Hurst would retreat to their London townhouse in the company of Caroline, while Anne and Georgiana would relocate from Netherfield to Longbourn for an extended stay. On more than one occasion, Mr Bennet was overheard jesting that the multitude of relocations had provoked such an increase in letter-writing that any raise in the cost of the postal service was entirely justified.

Mr Collins, having resumed his clerical duties, was held in high regard by his parishioners, who appreciated the transformation in his perspective. After extensive deliberation with Mr Bennet, he had resolved to remain in the living for an additional five years, after which he and Mary would retire to Longbourn, where their combined efforts would contribute to the estate's administration, ensuring that Mr Bennet's still-fragile health would not be overly taxed. Neither he nor Mary sought an extravagant honeymoon, as they agreed that the living itself would sufficiently provide for such amorous excursions.

Of all the couples, it was Elizabeth and Darcy who were the last to exchange vows. Darcy retained authority over Rosings until the Bingleys' return from their honeymoon, requiring several weeks to transfer control. While Bingley had competently managed Netherfield, the vastness of Rosings overwhelmed him initially.

Lord Fitzwilliam claimed second place, contending that the remoteness of his home and the arduousness of travelling there in inclement weather would render marriage an impracticality had he not promptly tied the knot upon the Bingleys' arrival. Therefore, he and his newly-wedded wife embarked on a honeymoon in Bath before returning to Hertfordshire to witness Mary's own nuptials.

Finally, as September neared its end, Elizabeth's wedding day appeared - accompanied by weather more delightful than customary for that time of year. Once again, Netherfield and Longbourn swarmed with visitors, among them the recently promoted General Fitzwilliam.

The specifics of the day eluded Elizabeth's memory as she chiefly recollected the intermingled anticipation and trepidation that preceded her union, the tender warmth of Darcy's grasp when he took her hand and the profound affection that radiated from their shared gazes.

Upon their return from a romantic honeymoon tour of the picturesque Lakes district, news reached them of General Fitzwilliam's engagement to Miss Charlotte Lucas. In his correspondence, Richard described Miss Lucas as a lady unlike any he had ever danced with—a pragmatic soul of remarkable distinction. This unexpected development left Darcy befuddled while Elizabeth revelled in unbridled delight, her laughter echoing with unrestrained mirth.

As for what followed, little remains to be recounted. In due course, Georgiana Darcy, Catherine Bennet, and Lydia Bennet found suitors who captured their hearts. Anne de Bourgh resided contentedly at Rosings, enjoying better health than she had ever known, living a respectable life as the cherished spinster aunt to the children of her beloved cousins.

In time, Lady Catherine de Bourgh grew reconciled to Janet's children. Though relations between them were never entirely free from tension, the strain eased, and her passing was met with genuine sorrow by all five Bennet sisters.

Mr and Mrs Bennet lived long enough to witness the marriages of many grandchildren before they departed this world within days of each other.

Darcy and Elizabeth, forever grateful for the happiness that graced their extended family, attributed it all to the serendipitous encounter that marked their initial meeting. It was when Lizzy boldly chastised both Darcy and Bingley for venturing into a meagre wilderness, thereby disturbing the tranquil sheep of Longbourn—a flock that, it must be noted, thrived and flourished, transforming Longbourn into an exceptionally prosperous estate.

Therefore, as the story draws to a close, the enduring legacy of love, resilience, and felicity intertwines with the rustic beauty of the English countryside, leaving an indelible mark on the lives of the Bennet sisters and their esteemed suitors. The echoes of their laughter, the tender embraces, and the gentle rustle of autumn leaves bear witness to the timeless enchantment that blossomed within the hallowed walls of Longbourn and continues to thrive for generations to come.

THE END

Made in the USA
Las Vegas, NV
10 December 2023

82461618R10105